DANE IN CHARGE

There were six of them: suntanned, husky-looking louts somewhere between eighteen and twenty-five.

I said, "Private island, guys. Load up and move out."

The leader of the pack spat on the sand. "You think you're big enough to make us?" he said.

I fired my shotgun into the nearest twelve-pack. When the sand blew away there was a heap of riddled cans and a puddle of cheap beer soaking slowly into the beach.

"Looks like he's big enough," one of them said at last.

HARDBALL

*An agent for hire
with a passion for justice*

HARDBALL

WILLIAM SANDERS

DIAMOND BOOKS, NEW YORK

HARDBALL

A Diamond Book/published by arrangement with
the author

PRINTING HISTORY
Diamond edition/January 1992

ISBN: 1-55773-645-6

Diamond Books are published by The Berkley Publishing Group,
200 Madison Avenue, New York, New York 10016.
The name "DIAMOND" and its logo are trademarks
belonging to Charter Communications Inc.

PRINTED IN THE UNITED STATES OF AMERICA

10 9 8 7 6 5 4 3 2 1

this one is for David
wado

HARDBALL

1

•••••

THEY SHOT ANOTHER BATCH OF PRISONERS THAT morning, an hour or so after daybreak. Probably they were supposed to do it at dawn, in the finest traditions of revolutionary justice. But this was Africa, where nothing ever happened on time since the first couple of hominids got into a rock fight over the hunting rights to the Olduvai Gorge.

They had been shooting prisoners about that time every day, all week, up against the mud-brick back wall of the inner courtyard. Even from the cell windows clear across the courtyard, you could see that the ground around the half-dozen wooden stakes was getting muddy with blood. On a quiet afternoon you could even hear the hum and drone of the swarming flies.

The executions weren't really much to see, as such things go; the local style tended to be pretty informal. The SS would have done it more efficiently, and Pancho Villa would have put more flair into it. Still, the job got done. . . .

There were twelve men in the firing squad. They might or might not have been the same twelve men each morning. They looked about like any other dozen members of the victorious Army of National Liberation: dented greenish helmets, ragged, too-big camouflage fatigues, and sweaty black faces with an expression that was somewhere between sullen boredom and no expression at all. From their unsteady gait they appeared to have been hitting the local booze—beer brewed from mealies, or maybe palm wine—not too many hours ago. That too was fairly standard operating procedure at these affairs.

They all carried AK-47 assault rifles. If today was like all the other days, the selector levers would be set to full automatic.

The firing squad sauntered into the courtyard, in no particular formation, and lined up roughly abreast, weapons pointing skyward. A big wooden door banged open and several more soldiers herded the prisoners into view.

There were only five prisoners today, three down from yesterday; five thin, haggard-looking black men, dressed in the tattered remnants of American-style olive-drab fatigues, their heads and feet bare. They shuffled along, looking down at the ground, making no effort to resist as the guards pushed and kicked them toward the line of head-high wooden stakes. Their features were too battered to show expressions but their gait and posture said all that needed to be said. They had gone past fear to a zombie-like resignation, maybe even a kind of relief at the prospect of getting it all over with. One man appeared to have wet himself, but the dark stain might have been blood.

There was no priest of any kind, no effort at prayer or other religious rites. Most of the rebels were Muslims from the coastal tribes, most of the defeated loyalists nominal Catholics and closet animists, but there was no God in this place. There was no nonsense with blindfolds, either, let alone cigarettes. The five men were tied quickly and roughly to the bullet-splintered stakes, hands bound behind their backs, and then the guards very sensibly got the hell out of there, glancing nervously over their shoulders at the firing squad.

Another door opened and a squat, wide-shouldered man, dressed in clean fatigues and a visored cap, stepped into the courtyard. He glanced at the prisoners, nodded once, and shouted a command.

The AK-47s came down and pointed. One of the prisoners suddenly sagged limply against the ropes that held him.

The officer shouted another order.

The AK-47s were on full-auto again today. The firing went on and on, a long sustained blast of automatic fire, the soldiers holding the triggers down and hosing the prisoners with 7.62mm bullets. It was a ridiculous amount of firepower to waste on five men at point-blank range, and yet the marksmanship was so bad that it took that much to do the job. Most of the jacketed slugs went into the wall, while the prisoners were hit repeatedly in legs and arms and lower body parts before the wild shots found vital targets. The noise was tremendous in the enclosed area.

When the firing stopped, four of the prisoners hung motionless against the ropes. The fifth, incredibly was still moving, his body jerking against the ropes, his feet kicking spasmodically at the bloody dirt.

The officer studied the fifth man for a moment and spat on the ground. He did not reach for his own holstered pistol. He called out something to the firing squad, sounding annoyed. Two of the soldiers walked over to the man who was still moving and pounded his head with their rifle butts until he was still.

Another day had begun in the Third World.

Everyone in the cell blocks had a fine view of the proceedings—everyone, at least, who was able to get up and look out the narrow, iron-barred windows that opened onto the courtyard. Of course there must have been a good many who couldn't, what with the friendly interrogation sessions and the untreated wounds from last week's street fighting, to say nothing of the dysentery that helped make the old French military prison such a fragrant place in the windless blast-furnace heat of a West African summer. . . . And no doubt there were others, physically capable of making it to the windows, who simply didn't give a damn anymore.

But everyone else watched. You could look out your own window and see them: the skinny black hands gripping the bars, the shadowy faces at the dark little openings in the shit-brown wall across the courtyard. And this even though it couldn't have been easy for a lot of them: the windows were so high that I could barely see out mine without stand-ing on tiptoe, and I was taller than most of the local men. The shorter prisoners must have had a hell of a time of it, pulling themselves up by the bars or taking turns lifting each other—there was nothing at all in the cells to stand on—but they did whatever they had to do, and they watched.

Some of them must have been looking for friends or relatives among the victims, and others might have been trying to imagine what it would be like when their numbers came up. For most it was probably just something to help pass the time. There was little else to break the monotony of the long hours between beatings and electric shocks to the scrotum and other officially scheduled recreations.

I used to think that maybe that was the one small conso-lation in the situation: when your own turn came to stand there and exchange stares with a dozen of Kalashnikov's fine products, at least you could reflect that you were helping provide a little entertainment in a place that was notably short on laughs.

I had an unusually good seat, so to speak, for the daily shootings. My cell was up on the second floor and midway down the east side of the quadrangle, opposite the execution stakes—which had been thoughtfully placed so that the firing squad wouldn't have the morning sun in their eyes; a practical bit of planning, considering how bad the shooting was under the best of circumstances. I wondered sometimes how many governments had gotten rid of their enemies against that wall. The country had had at least a dozen since the French left back in the sixties.

Actually my accommodations could have been a lot worse in several respects. For one thing, I had a cell all to myself, which was a rare luxury in that place. From what I'd seen through the cell doors on my way to and from the Commandant's office, most of the cells on both floors were crammed and packed like chicken coops. True, the daily executions must be gradually improving the space situation—together with the occasional truckloads of prisoners hauled off to unspecified destinations—but there was still a long way to go.

I suppose some people might have found the solitude hard to take, but it was fine with me: this wasn't the first time I'd occupied a solitary cell, and I'd never had any trouble with that part of it. I've always been happier on my own anyway. There was a Company shrink who tried to make something out of that, once, but I never did figure out what was eating him. If God wanted people to have other people around all the time, he'd have made everybody Siamese twins.

The cell itself was pretty much like all the others in the old mud-brick prison, though, at least as far as I could tell. Six feet by ten—God knows I paced it off enough times—and about eight feet from floor to ceiling, the room was almost totally bare. There had once been some sort of bunk or cot, judging from the markings on the wall where bolts had been removed; now, though, the only furniture was the rusty and slightly leaky bucket that served as the toilet. (Now and then somebody even remembered to come empty it.) That was it. The only personal possessions in the cell were the filthy shorts and T-shirt I lived in. The highly occasional meals were brought around in an unwashed tin pan, from which you ate with your fingers or not at all, and the pan was taken away immediately afterward.

The door was made of thick iron bars, scabby with rust. All I could see across the corridor, no matter where I stood or how hard I mashed my face against the bars, was a solid blank wall. There were people in the cells on either side of me; I heard them moving around and muttering at night, despite the strict no-talking rules. I could have tried to speak with them—I didn't know the local language, but some of them might have known French or Arabic—but there was nothing they could do for me, nothing they could know that I needed to learn, and the poor bastards would have gotten an extra beating or worse if they'd been caught talking with the white American.

I take back what I said, though; I did have cellmates, quite a few of them. Most of them seemed to have six legs—and yes, by God, I caught them and I counted, more than once; in a situation like that you do anything to occupy your mind. They bit like tiny pit bulls and probably carried various nasty tropical diseases, too, but right now that wasn't a priority worry. . . . There were no rats for some reason, but there was a big spotted lizard that came in through the window now and then looking for flies. He came to the right place. So far I hadn't given him a name or started talking to him, but it could only be a matter of time.

Assuming, of course, that I was going to have any more time. There was always that.

Not exactly the Hilton, all in all. Still, after the recent demonstration of one of the likelier alternatives, I didn't feel I ought to complain. And after the nightly visits to the Commandant's office, the cell looked pretty good to me.

But of course it couldn't last much longer. It did seem that my luck, or time, or something, had just about run out.

The hell of it was, they really did have me all wrong this time. For once I was a genuinely innocent bystander—well, innocent of anything in their territory, anyway—who just happened to be ambushed by events.

I hadn't even known what was going on in their squalid little country; the day I got off the once-a-week plane at the tiny airport outside the capital, I couldn't have told you the name of their president, and two days before that I'd have had trouble finding the place on a map of Africa. I certainly didn't have any interest in their internal affairs. There are any number of vicious civil wars going on all over Africa at any given time, most of them unreported by the international press—as long as no important Westerners get hurt—and you could go crazy trying to keep track of them all. If I'd had any idea that the rebels were about to win their war, I'd have stayed far away from the whole country.

I was there on a private mission, looking for a man I had known some years ago, a man I needed for a job I was trying to put together in another part of the world. I had an address and a report that he was employed by the government, training and organizing security forces. It was a long way to come for one man, but he was extremely good at certain specialized tasks, and the people for whom I was putting the operation together were very insistent.

I never did find him. The rebel blitz began just before sunrise on my first day in the country, and the capital fell

before I could even find the address that was all I had to
go on.

Naturally nobody believed any of this. There was the tim-
ing of my arrival, and there was my association with a foreign advisor to the fallen government—they'd learned from
the hotel staff that I'd been making inquiries and trying to
make phone calls. And then there was the indisputable fact
that nobody in the world would visit their hell-hole capital
without powerful and pressing reasons, especially in early
summer and in the middle of a revolution. Christ, if I'd
been in their place I'd have drawn the same conclusions;
I'd have had me shot long before this.

And if they succeeded in finding out anything at all
about my personal and professional background—which
they would, sooner or later; they were too well armed and
equipped not to have some sort of outside-world contacts—
it was going to be all over.

I should, I thought as I moved away from the window,
have listened to my mother when she wanted me to take
piano lessons. I could be sitting somewhere in a nice cool
bar right now, a tall and very cold drink close at hand,
playing a medley of Billy Joel hits for admiring and horny
ladies in clinging evening wear. . . .

Booted feet banged and clomped in the corridor. A couple of guards appeared outside the barred door, looking in
at me. The nearer one said in barely comprehensible French,
"You. White man. Commandant says you come now."

So the little bastard wanted to have a morning session
today. I sighed to myself, feeling the assorted aches and
burns and bruises from last night's discussion, and stood
back from the door while the guard got out his keys. As
he struggled with the rusty old lock, the other man poked
the muzzle of his AK-47 through the bars, covering me. It
was a pretty pointless thing to do. The shape I was in by

now, I couldn't have jumped a gradeschool crossing guard. But they both watched me nervously, keeping their weapons ready all the way down the corridor, down the narrow spiral stairs and across the courtyard to the Commandant's office.

The Commandant was seated at his desk when they hustled me in. He was a skinny, hyped-up little son of a bitch with a patch over one eye, sort of a cross between Sammy Davis Junior and a spitting cobra. He smiled at me, friendly as a barbed-wire fence.

"Good news," he said in French. "Someone is here to take you away. We will miss you."

I wasn't really listening to him. I was looking at the tall blond-haired man in the tan tropical suit who stood beside the Commandant's desk, looking at me with an odd expression, as if he'd been expecting me but I didn't quite fit the picture in his mind.

"Our little conversations," the Commandant added, "have meant so much to me. You'll never know."

The white man stepped forward and stuck out his hand. "Good morning, Mr. Dane," he said in accented but excellent English. "As the Commandant says, I'm here to get you out of this place. An aircraft is waiting."

I took his hand automatically, while my mind tried to grapple with what he was saying. Out of here? I'd almost forgotten there was anywhere else.

He said, "My name is Somov, Mr. Dane. You may call me Vladimir."

On the way to the airport Vladimir said, "Forgive me for staring, Mr. Dane. It's only that you don't much resemble the description I was given."

The car hit a pothole and bounced hard, throwing us both off balance in the back seat. The driver said, "*Izvinitye.*"

"Embassy driver," Vladimir said to me, as if that explained something. "As I was saying. . . ." He looked me up and down with his pale blue eyes. "I suppose the height is about right—six feet, isn't it? I have trouble with your English measurements. But I was led to expect a man, ah, somewhat more heavily built. And if you'll forgive my saying so, Mr. Dane, right now you look considerably older than forty years."

He shook his head, looking worried. "*Bozhe moi*, did they treat you so badly in there, to change you so much in such a short time? Or was I simply given incorrect information?"

I said, "I've been sick."

He laughed. "Ah, the old American joke. I have heard it before."

Actually that was no joke. The truth was that I'd been in bad shape before I ever bought a ticket for this particular corner of Hell; I'd been pushing myself, kidding myself, for a long time now.

I'd been poking around some of the unhealthiest spots on the planet for a lot of years, mostly Africa and the Middle East with a few Southeast Asian digressions. I'd been shot and beaten up, chewed on by various bugs, soaked in monsoons and dehydrated in deserts. I'd missed a lot of meals and eaten others I should have left alone; I'd drunk water you wouldn't wash a dog in and booze that they should have left in the camel. I'd had malaria and dengue fever and God knows what else . . . and all the time I'd kept telling myself it didn't matter, get on with the job, finish the mission, swallow a handful of pills and ignore the chills and the shaking and the pains, once the job was done I could check into a clinic somewhere . . . but of course I never did. There was always another job waiting, something else requiring me to run off to some other place that nobody in his right mind would go.

And you can do that sort of thing to yourself when you're young and stupid and maybe you can get away with it for a while, but I was hitting forty this year and it was starting to catch up with me.

But all I said was, "I'm surprised the KGB has any information on me at all. I wouldn't have thought I rated a file."

Vladimir laughed again, sounding really amused this time. "Mr. Dane, I don't even know whether the KGB has a file on you or not. The description I was given," he said, watching my face, "was provided by your own Central Intelligence Agency."

My face must have done some strange things; he was laughing hard now, one of those big open-mouthed Russian laughs, coming up from way down in the chest. "Yes," he said happily after a minute or so, "I thought you would react to that. What did you think—that you were being spirited away to the Soviet Union for some sinister purpose?"

He patted me gently on the shoulder. "Relax, Mr. Dane. This is merely a little goodwill gesture on the part of my organization. We live in a new era," he said with only the lightest touch of sarcasm, "perestroika and glasnost and all that. For now, at least, official policy is to foster better relations, even at the secret-agency level. Here and there, we help one another in small ways that do no harm."

He looked out the window at the passing landscape. We were crossing a flat dusty plain, where nothing grew taller than the waist-high thornbushes. Alongside the dirt road lay the wreckage of several burned-out military trucks.

He was silent for a moment; he seemed to have gone somewhere else in his mind. I looked him over carefully for the first time. He was about my age, I guessed, maybe a few years older; the nearly white hair would have hidden any streaks of gray. He was a little taller than me, with a long thin face—"aristocratic" was a word that came to mind, though it seemed inappropriate to describe a Soviet agent—and if he'd been any lighter he'd have been an albino. I wondered how he coped with the African sun; he didn't have a hat with him, yet his face wasn't sunburned. Maybe he didn't get out much in the daylight.

"A new era," he repeated at last. "This sort of thing—" He waved a long-fingered hand at the blackened wrecks by the roadside, a gesture that somehow took in the whole country and its current affairs. "Once we went in heavily for sponsoring such goings-on. No more. We are rapidly going out of the revolution business—or at least becoming much more selective about our clients. It was never a very profitable business, on the whole. But we had our share of the sort of people you call 'cowboys.' "

He chuckled. "Still, we do try to at least keep an eye on these little affairs, just on—what is the idiom?" He snapped his fingers. "On general principles, yes. A few cases of AK-47s, a few advisors, all in all a cheap price to pay for information and influence in situations that might one day make trouble for us. And old habits die hard in secret agencies."

I said, "So I've noticed."

"I'd imagine you have. I think you and I could probably exchange some interesting stories. At any rate," he said, "it was conveyed to us that a man named Dane was being held prisoner by the victorious Army of National Liberation, and that the Americans would be grateful if we could use our influence to have him released."

I said, "And the other half of the deal? I mean, just how grateful is the Company supposed to be?"

"Now, now. Even if I had that information—which I don't; we too observe the 'need to know' principle—you know better than to ask. No doubt there will be something, a small favor for a small favor. As you say, it's no big deal." He frowned. "Is that right? 'No big deal'? American expressions fascinate me."

We were getting close to the airport now. I could see the concrete control tower rising out of the plain.

"And I'm afraid that's all I can tell you," Vladimir said. "I wish we had more time to talk, but my orders are to put you on the airplane immediately."

"Where's the plane going?"

"I'm not sure, actually. Morocco, I think. At any rate, you'll be met there by someone from your agency."

I said, "If you mean the CIA, it's not my agency."

"So I understand. Hasn't been for a long time, anyway. You're something of a private entrepreneur, aren't you, Mr. Dane? Doing contract work for various parties and persons, including but not limited to the secret agencies of the United States. What they call a free lance."

He grinned. "Do you know the origin of that expression, by the way? In medieval times, it meant that a knight was available for service with whatever king or lord cared to employ him. His lance was free for hire."

I didn't reply. I closed my eyes and leaned back against the upholstery. It was the softest thing I'd felt in over a week.

I wondered who the Company was sending to pick me up, and whether it would be somebody I knew. I wondered, too, what they were going to want. If they had another job in mind, they could forget it.

It was time to take my lance back home for awhile. It was getting bent and rusted all to hell.

2
. . . . .

CAMERON SAID, "I DON'T KNOW, DANE. A MAN like you in a job like this—seems kind of a waste. You sure you want to do this?"

I said, "You know something, Cameron? In all these years, I think that's the first time anybody from the Company asked me that."

"Yeah," he said. "I guess it probably is."

He took off his straw hat and leaned on one of the boat dock pilings and looked out across the blue waters of the bay, toward the distant blurry line of the mainland. The sun was bouncing off the wave tops in little points of light, so bright it hurt your eyes.

"Got a nice view here, anyway," he said. "Ought to be some good fishing, if you like that kind of thing. The hell am I trying to talk you out of it for? I wouldn't mind spending a couple of months on this island myself, if they'd let me leave the old lady at home."

He rubbed his bald head. "Sun's sure as hell hot, though. But I guess after Africa and those raghead countries this must not feel like much to you."

He was a heavy-set man, somewhere in his middle sixties I guessed. He had a round red face and freckled arms and white eyebrows; he had on a short-sleeved white shirt and baggy tan slacks and white canvas shoes, and he looked pretty much like a damn old fool. I knew a little about his record, though. He hadn't always been the local CIA man in a backwater office on the Texas coast. And he definitely wasn't any kind of a fool.

I said, "It'll do fine. This is exactly what I need for awhile."

"Got some recovering to do? Well, this ought to be a good place for it, all right. Come on," he said, turning and starting back along the dock. "I'll show you around."

The boat dock seemed fairly new, but the planks were already starting to warp and curl in the Gulf Coast sun. Our footsteps made loud rattling noises as we walked.

"Pretty rough, was it?" Cameron said. "Africa, I mean. That last business."

"Rough enough. Could have been worse," I said. "Not as bad as some spots I could remember." Not as bad as some Cameron had been in, for sure: I'd seen the report on what they'd done to him in Rumania. But I wasn't supposed to know about that, so I didn't say anything.

He said, "The rebels were Muslims, weren't they? Good thing they didn't know you were the one who whacked Abdelkader."

I stopped and swung around to face him, so fast he took a step backward and almost went off the dock. "Jesus Christ, Cameron. Shut up about that, will you?"

He looked up at me for a moment, his face puzzled. "Well, yeah, I guess you're right, really shouldn't talk about classified stuff—of course there's nobody on the island but the two of us, and it's miles to the nearest land, but still I suppose there could be some kind of bugs. . . ."

Then his face cleared. "Oh, hell, I get you now. You mean shut up about it as in you don't want to talk about it, period. That it?"

I nodded. Cameron said, "Shit, Dane, I'm sorry. Don't

know why it didn't occur to me you might have, well, problems about that hit—" He raised both hands as I started to speak. "Okay, okay. No more talk about—that business we won't talk about. Forget I said anything."

We started walking again. From the dock you could see most of what there was to see on the north end of the island: a narrow strip of beach, a lot of high white dunes with clumps of tall grasses growing on top, and, rising above the dunes a short way inland, the upper part of a white-painted house. Or cottage, I suppose it would have been called in a real-estate description.

"Interesting history to this little retreat," Cameron said. "Used to be owned by this fairly big-time drug operator who used it for his home away from Houston, as well as obvious business purposes. When the DEA finally busted him they confiscated the property, as usual—"

"They can do that?"

"Hell, Dane, you been out of the country too long. They can do damn near *anything*, once they say that magic word 'drugs.' You're gonna be real surprised at some of the changes in this country . . . anyway," he said as we climbed toward the house, "the DEA did some kind of deal with their brother agency and now the Company owns this place. Use it for various things—meetings, planning sessions, stashing the occasional defector, or sometimes high-level officers just come down here to relax and fish and fuck off for a few days. Sort of like those dachas the KGB owns outside Moscow, you know?"

The house was at the top of a rise of ground, maybe thirty or forty feet above water level. Even so, the house itself had been built on high, solid-looking pilings, raising it a good ten feet more above the sandy ground. It wasn't all that big a house, now I could see the whole thing: just a square wooden box, about fifty feet to a side, with a wide redwood sun deck running around the outside. Plenty big enough for a week of fooling around, but you wouldn't have wanted to raise a family in it. The windows were covered by large sheets of unpainted plywood. The paint on the outside walls appeared to be fairly recent, which was a relief. I'd been wondering if my duties were supposed to include repainting the damn thing.

Cameron gestured at the miniature forest of heavy pilings beneath the house. "Somebody did a hell of a job there," he said. "Every now and then, when there's a big enough storm off the Gulf, the water comes right over these little islands. I know it looks like a long way up, but that isn't shit when the Gulf gets on a tear, believe me. It hasn't happened since this place was built, but it's going to, sooner or later. So they built for it."

He kicked at the white sand underfoot. "Not that it's going to make any difference in the long run. All these Texas coastal islands are nothing but sand and shell and a little rotting driftwood and bird shit. One of these days there's going to be a really serious hurricane, and when it's over you'll have to hunt hard to find any sign of any of this." He waved his hand at the house. "Going to just wipe all this fancy shit off the island, maybe take the island out too."

He looked out to seaward, where the low-lying shape of a long island cut across the mouth of the big blue bay. "This isn't as bad a spot as some," he said. "You're in the bay rather than open water, and the barrier islands break some of the force of the storm. Still, if they put out a hurricane warning, you get your ass out of here. Shit," he said, "only a dope-dealing yuppie would spend that kind of money on a place that's on borrowed time from the first storm. Well, it's not your problem. Or his, any more."

In back of the house, some distance away, sat a good-sized concrete-block structure, nearly as big as the house itself. It was ugly as hell but it looked solid. Cameron said, "Now there you got a little more realistic thinking. Generator's down at one end—I'll show you how to get it started before I leave—and there's a storage room that takes up the rest of the thing. Got tools and stuff in there now, but it used to be where they stashed the dope. The son of a bitch might have been crazy but he wasn't completely stupid, he wasn't going to risk having a storm surge dump salt water over half a million bucks' worth of Colombian nose powder. Damn thing's built like one of those Nazi bunkers."

I wasn't paying very close attention. I was looking at another structure I hadn't even seen from the water—looking at it, but not necessarily believing it. I said, "What the hell?"

Cameron looked around and saw what I was staring at. "Oh, right," he said. "Looks weird, doesn't it? I forgot to tell you."

Down among the dunes, perhaps a hundred yards from the house, an ordinary house trailer sat on some sort of blocks. It was a bit bigger than the usual vacation trailer, but not quite big enough to be called a "mobile home"; it was a shiny natural metal color all over, and the shell was rounded and streamlined rather than the usual boxy shape. It looked as if the wheels had been removed.

Anywhere else, it would have been a sight too ordinary even to notice. On a dinky island with salt water on all sides and nothing resembling a road, it looked bizarre enough to serve as some experimental artist's statement on the absurdity of life. I wondered if the previous owner of the island had been sampling too much of his own goods.

Cameron said, "I have the impression this was where they

lived until they got the house built. There's an old man over on the mainland, runs this boat dock, says they took the whole thing off its wheels and put it on some pontoons and just floated it out here on a calm day, towing it behind a motorboat. Winched it up here, I guess, and it's been here ever since. Must be the only trailer in Texas on an island. Of course, the first serious hurricane, this thing's done for, but so far it's stayed put. They got it anchored fairly solid."

He tilted his head and grinned at me. "You better get to liking it, Dane. That's going to be your living quarters."

"My what? I thought—"

"Thought you'd be staying in the main house? Dream on, Dane. You may have some old war buddies in the Company with enough clout to fix you up with a little sandbagging job while you get your shit back together, but you're still just a no-rank free lance. And this is strictly for the upper classes, son." He jerked his thumb at the house. "Only the baboons with the biggest, reddest asses get to occupy this little bungalow. We're talking perks here."

"Son of a bitch."

"Now, now, it's not so bad. You'll see. Inside of that trailer's fixed up pretty good—TV, VCR, stereo, first-class little kitchen. Did have a satellite dish out here, but the last storm got it . . . and you can help yourself to stuff from the house," Cameron said, "within reason of course. Booze from the bar—oh, yeah, it's got one—video and music tapes, whatever, long as you don't get too damn blatant about it. Chances are nobody's going to be using the place the whole time you're here anyway. Besides," he added, "the house is all boarded up, probably got a lot of stuff needs to be done before you could use it. The trailer's ready to move into right now."

He leaned against the nearest piling and looked me up and down. "Look, Dane," he said, "nobody really expects you to do much around here. You and I both know this is just a bullshit job, something to give you a couple of months to recover, because some people figure they owe you. All anybody wants you to do is keep an eye on the place—we've had some trouble with wild-ass kids coming over from the mainland, little vandalism, little theft, nothing big—and do a little low-level maintenance now and then. Beyond that, you can spend your days lying in the sun playing with yourself for all we care."

I said, "Any weapons on the place?"

I don't know why I asked that. Force of habit, I guess.

Cameron gave me a sharp look. "Don't know what you'd need with weapons," he said slowly, "but I think there's a shotgun in the house. If you're thinking about the kids I mentioned, try not to actually shoot any of them. The local authorities have been told this place is restricted U.S. government property and secret as all hell, and they've always been completely cooperative—I mean, Christ, this is Texas, we could probably set off a small atom bomb out here and they'd pretend not to notice—but we'd rather not do anything to force them to take an interest."

He took a ring of keys out of his pocket and nodded toward the redwood stairway that led up to the house.

"Come on," he said. "I'll show you the whole place."

Late in the afternoon we took the skiff back across the two-and-a-half-mile channel to the mainland. I held the skiff's blunt metal bow against the dilapidated old dock while Cameron climbed stiffly up the rusty iron ladder. At the top he turned and looked down at me and grinned. "Take it easy, now," he said. "You have any problems, give me a call. There's a radiotelephone in the house. I understand every now and then it even works, but that may just be a rumor."

I said, "I'll be all right."

"Oh, sure. I've read your file, Dane. I remember you, too, when you were with the Company full time. We never met, but I saw a lot of reports . . . and there's no doubt in my mind you'll be all right. Still, you've got that number I gave you," he said. "You get too lonesome, call me and I'll see if I can get Acquisition and Disbursement to buy you one of those inflatable women."

The dock was too high for us to shake hands, so we settled for exchanging waves. I backed the skiff away from the dock and turned slowly seaward, handling the big outboard's throttle with probably excessive caution—it had been years since I'd operated any sort of small boat—and when I looked back Cameron was already waddling down the dock toward his car.

I fed the Johnson gas and the skiff began to pick up speed, the bow rising and starting to plane, the light choppy waves banging and thumping against the flat metal bottom, the big prop kicking up a rooster-tail plume of sparkling spray. It felt good to be out on the water on a sunny day, driving a piece of powerful machinery and going fast for no reason at all, nowhere to be in a hurry and nobody chasing me or shooting at me, just running hard for the hell of it.

It felt good to be alone.

A lot has been said about the CIA, and God knows I've said my share and more. But you have to give it to the Company: when they do get it together, they can be damn impressive.

It had been three weeks now since I'd said my goodbyes to what they used to call the Dark Continent. Much of that time had been spent in a Company medical center near Washington D.C., getting a thorough going-over by some unnervingly efficient people in white coats.

I remembered one doctor, a pleasant though cold-fingered young guy with an impressive set of sun-bleached California eyebrows, who said, "You know, Dane, people have been hanged for war crimes for doing to other people the things you've done to yourself. If human bodies came with a warranty, you'd have voided yours long ago."

Their final conclusion, to everyone's surprise, was that there wasn't all that much wrong with me, though they were damned if they could figure out why. All I really needed, it seemed, was a little peace and quiet and rest.

The doctoring hadn't cost me a thing—and I'd guess all those tests would have added up to a bone-crunching bill in any civilian hospital—and, within a couple of days of the final report, the Company had come through with this little caretaker job on a Texas coastal island. All this even though I hadn't been part of the CIA, except on occasional contract jobs, for over a decade. As Cameron had said, certain influential people in higher Company echelons went pretty far back with me, and evidently they did feel they, or the Company, owed me something.

Of course in a highly indirect sense I'd been working for the Company at the time I got imprisoned, but that wouldn't have cut a quarter's worth of ice in itself. That just isn't how it works. . . .

True, I didn't entirely buy this heart-warming little scenario. Some day, some way, I was going to get some kind of a bill for this. It might be years; then again, they might already have something in mind for me to do for them—but one way or another, it would come around. Because now I owed them.

Back on the island, I tied the skiff up at the dock, climbed the board walkway, and started toward the trailer. Then I thought of something and changed direction, digging in my pocket for the keys Cameron had given me.

There was a tall walnut cabinet in the bedroom of the house; I'd noticed it on our little tour of inspection, but Cameron hadn't said anything about it and I hadn't asked. The smallest key on the ring unlocked it, as I'd guessed, and, sure enough, it did contain the shotgun Cameron had mentioned. There were racks for a couple more guns, but they were empty.

I took the piece out and looked it over. A fairly cheap-looking pump shotgun, without any fancy engraving or extra features, it bore a brand name I didn't recognize. It was a mere 20-gauge, light and handy and good for small game birds such as quail, but not much use for anything bigger unless you got in close and used the largest size shot. Or slugs; that would turn it into a fairly decent weapon, I supposed. There were several boxes of shells in a drawer beneath the main compartment, and I took one out and opened it.

The ammunition was even more of a disappointment. Nothing but Number Eight shot, tiny little pellets the size of birdseed, capable of pissing a grown man off if you shot him with it, and not much else. Another drawer provided the explanation, in the form of a few boxes of clay pigeons and a hand trap. Somebody had thought it might be fun to spend an afternoon doing a little informal skeet shooting down on the beach; the gun wasn't meant as a weapon in any sense. Well, I should have known they wouldn't leave anything really lethal in an empty house on a deserted coastal island.

I stood there for a minute, holding the shotgun in one hand and a bunch of those ridiculous birdshot shells in the other, trying to think what the hell I'd wanted with a gun in the first place. It wasn't as if I felt naked without one, like some pulp-story hero; I'd gone for long periods in the field, sometimes in genuinely dangerous places and among armed enemies, with no hardware more potent than a pocketknife, because sometimes carrying a gun gets you into more trouble than it can get you out of.

All the same, in the end, I tucked the shotgun under my arm and crammed a few shells into my pockets. What the hell, I might get attacked by a crazed sandpiper. Or the island might be invaded by a pack of bloodthirsty little clay discs. You never know.

On the way out I thought of something else, went over to the little bar, unlocked the under-the-counter cabinet, and issued myself a fifth of Jim Beam. Unlike the shotgun, this was something I was fairly sure I was going to need.

Armed and provisioned against almost any contingency, I went back down the stairs and across the sandy flat to my trailer. It was starting to get dark, the sun already almost out of sight in a bloody blaze over the Texas mainland, and I realized suddenly that I still hadn't had my supper.

. . . The ground up on the hillside was hard and studded with sharp rocks and cactus spines. I took off my desert-camo bush jacket and folded it to make a pad for my elbows and then reached again for the big rifle.

I got into the sling, hauling the oiled leather tight against my forearm, and socketed the butt pad into my shoulder, locking the rifle into a solid unit with the tripod base of elbows and upper body. The smooth wood of the stock felt cool and comfortable against my cheek as I snuggled my face into position and peered into the reticle of the long Bushnell scope. Everything was done slowly and deliberately; there was all the time in the world, right up until the shot, but if that went wrong the time would run out permanently.

The high-magnification scope yanked everything close. Suddenly I was no longer lying on a hillside looking at a cluster of houses almost a quarter of a mile away, I was standing practically on the doorstep of the house I wanted. When an old woman in a black *chadoor* came out the door, carrying a hefty-looking basket, I could see the wrinkles on her face above the black veil.

The watch on my wrist beeped very softly, letting me know it was time. Or close, anyway; the people down in the village probably didn't have precisely accurate clocks—but they wouldn't be far off. Not much else in the Middle East happens on time, but prayer time for the faithful is a serious matter. And this was Abdelkader's turf, where slackness in religious observances would not be tolerated.

And, of course, where Abdelkader himself always led afternoon prayers in person at the village mosque. . . .

The white-robed figure appeared in the doorway so suddenly that my pulse went up for a second. Even though I'd been waiting for him, even after all the pictures and films I'd studied and the times I'd seen him in person at a distance, he startled me. The dark, white-bearded face wore a look of such intensity, the eyes stared straight in my direction with such burning power, that I had to remind myself he couldn't possibly see me. It wasn't just that the rocks and the cacti hid me from the village, and the sun was at my back; Abdelkader was blind.

He stood in the doorway a moment, perhaps feeling the sun on his face. His hands went up and made a small adjustment to the famous black turban. His mouth opened; he seemed to be speaking to someone. I thought he might be calling for the young boy who usually led him around.

The rifle's safety snicked silently off under my thumb. The trigger came back until all the slack was out and the ball of my finger began to meet resistance. The crosshairs were steady on the center of the target.

The trigger released with the brittle suddenness of a

glass rod breaking. The big rifle surged rather than kicked against my shoulder, the recoil of the handloaded Magnum cartridge absorbed by the massive custom stock and the extra-heavy barrel. I didn't hear it go off. You never do, if your concentration has been right.

Abdelkader stood in the doorway. Nothing in the scene had changed except that there was now a splash of red, not particularly big, on the front of the white robe, square in the middle of his chest. Contrary to legend, the heart is not on the left side.

He was still facing in my direction, still seeming to look straight at me.

I threw down the rifle—it had done its job, it was too heavy to run with, and getting caught with it would have been much worse than fatal—and began to scramble away, back up the mountainside toward the dirt road and the waiting car. I could see the white shape in the doorway even without the scope, the white robe flaring out around him as he fell. The echo of the shot came racketing back up the hillside. People were starting to pour out of the other houses.

But part of my mind was still stuck in time, still seeing that face in the scope: and all the way down the mountain road, through the mad, high-speed run for the coast road and then the welcome anonymity of the streets of Beirut, I kept seeing those terrible sightless eyes staring into mine above the crosshairs. . . .

I sat up in bed and threw the tangled sheet off my legs and said, "Shit."

I sat there for a moment, getting back into myself. When you've awakened in the middle of the night in enough strange places with the same flashback dream, sometimes you have to think to remember where you are this time around. Then the sound of the waves on the beach came through the windows of the trailer.

I got up and stretched and looked at my watch. Four in the morning. Right on time. No way I was going to get back to sleep any time soon, either; I knew how it worked.

I punched the radio on and let it play while I groped my way into the trailer's tiny kitchen and opened the refrigerator. There was plenty of beer, along with the rest of the provisions Cameron and I had brought out that day. I popped open a can of Lone Star and went back and sat on the bed, listening to a song on the radio.

George Jones, no mistaking that industrial-strength whisky tenor, was telling about a man whose wife had taken off, leaving him with nothing but a bottle of whisky shaped like Elvis Presley and an empty Fred Flintstone jelly-bean jar for a drinking glass. So he sits there getting drunker and drunker and talking with Elvis and Fred about women and life.

You couldn't beat real hard-core country music, I thought as the beer trickled down my throat, at a time like this; maybe it was corny and tacky at times and maybe ninety percent of the songs had the same four-chord changes, but it was the definitive alone-at-four-in-the-morning-and-can't-sleep sound. Rock lyrics, when they said anything at all, were about young people finding out for the first time that life could be confusing or outright shitty. Country songs were about grown-up people who had blown their options.

George Jones's voice said: *it's all fucked up and it ain't going to get any better, but what the hell, let's have another one.*

The song ended and, a moment later, the radio speakers rumbled with the first notes of a walking-bass piano run that I hadn't heard in years. Jerry Lee Lewis, for God's sake; nothing else in the world sounded remotely like that

rolling-thunder left hand. The country stations seemed to
be playing a good deal of the older rock stuff nowadays,
especially the old Memphis bunch. No doubt the people
who listened to country stations now, the waitresses and
factory hands and gas pumpers and truck drivers, were the
same ones who had listened to Elvis and Roy and Jerry
Lee and Carl back when they were kids.

I didn't think the radio stations' demographic studies
took note of the tastes of insomniac ex-CIA cowboys. But
I might be wrong; they can do some pretty detailed break-
downs nowadays. . . . Maybe they ought to approach, oh,
Smith & Wesson or the Uzi people about buying some
commercial time.

I closed my eyes for a moment, enjoying the cold beer
and the music. It was one of Jerry Lee's later songs, with
that underlying edge of walking-wounded knowledge that
must have come out of getting thrown down and gang-raped
by the same hype-hustlers that had put him on top in the
first place. The ever-vigilant Hypocrite Brigade had been
on one of their periodic offensives, and the industry needed
a sacrificial victim to throw to the menopausal wolf pack—
and Elvis, who was also putting it to a teenage girl at about
the same time, represented too big an investment to dump.
So Elvis got to be the certified Fine American Boy and
the Killer found himself turned overnight into a human
plague ship.

Maybe that was one reason I always liked the guy so
much. In my line of work, you get to know a lot about
betrayals and sellouts in the interest of the Big Picture.
Of course you could also make something, if you wanted,
out of my fondness for a singer who was called the Killer.
You could go fuck yourself too.

This one was a song I hadn't heard before: "Thirty-Nine
and Holding," about a man making a fool of himself with

younger women while he fights against the onset of middle age. Maybe that was what I was doing in my own way, I reflected, finishing the beer and tossing the can in no particular direction. Maybe the craziness of my life, in the last few years, came from nothing more dignified than an inability to cope with the transition from thirty-something to forty-some-odd. The guy in the song seemed to be having a lot more fun, but what did I know?

After a couple of minutes I went and got the Jim Beam. I wasn't supposed to be drinking at all. There were some little yellow pills I was supposed to be taking, and the Company doctor had been very emphatic about the dangers of mixing them with alcohol. But I figured that was easy to take care of; I'd just give up little yellow pills.

Right now I knew what I needed most.

3

• • • • •

THE ISLAND WAS A LITTLE LESS THAN TWO MILES long and maybe half to three-quarters of a mile across at its fattest point. About halfway down its length there was a narrow little neck where the sea was working away at turning it into two small islands. It looked to me as if another big hurricane or two would do the job, but I didn't really know anything about such things.

As Cameron had said, it was nothing but a pile of sand and shell, covered with those long funny-looking grasses called "sea-oats" and a few clumps of low, wind-twisted live-oak trees. It was really more of a big sandbar than an island; there are no true islands off the Texas coast, just those long skinny sand formations, strung out along the coastline from Galveston clear down to the Mexican border, all of them piled up by millions of years of wave action and rivers washing sand down from the far-off Texas interior. Some of them actually had paved roads and real-estate developments and even fair-sized towns. This struck me as somewhat crazy, but no more so than a lot of other things I'd seen since coming back to the States.

The one I was occupying—it didn't seem to have a name; at least none was shown on the detailed marine maps on the wall of the trailer—sat roughly in the middle of a big shallow bay. A string of long barrier islands protected it from the worst of the Gulf storms, which was probably why the whole ridiculous thing hadn't disappeared long ago like some kind of midget Atlantis. Even so, one good look around convinced me that if a serious hurricane ever blew up, I was going to sit it out in a motel as far inland as I could get.

This had once been a pretty active area, a popular and busy port for fishermen, pirates, slavers, and, for a little while, Confederate blockade runners. But the bay had gradually silted up and now the only town still in business on the bay was Bayport: a Mom and Pop grocery-and-gas stop, a scattering of ratty little houses and a few trailers up on blocks, and a nearly derelict motel that apparently survived off the occasional sport-fishing party. There was also the boat dock where a mysterious old man still did some business renting boats and selling bait, and some ruined docks and abandoned warehouses from a long-gone time of prosperity. The nearest real town was a place called Soto, eighteen miles up the coast by a really bad blacktop road.

Long ago, this area had been inhabited by the Karankawa Indians, an extremely low-rent tribe that had probably been pushed out onto the sand islands by tougher and smarter mainland bands. They hadn't done very well for themselves. Their canoe technology was too poor for effective sea fishing, and there wasn't much of a variety of food available on the islands, and pretty soon they were too inbred to think of ways to improve their situation. They hadn't hit it off at all with the early white settlers of the area, who didn't exactly represent a high point in human evolution themselves, and war broke out almost immediately. Partly this was because the Karankawas supplemented their diet by eating strange humans who happened along, and partly it might have been because they were, by all accounts, just about the ugliest and most disagreeable bunch of Indians God ever let live. As far as anyone knew there were none of them left and nobody missed them, not even other Indians.

I learned all this fascinating information from a collection of books I found in the main house, mostly badly-written, privately-printed efforts by some local amateur historian. Or rather I got the history and the geography from the book-shelf. The physical description of the island was something I picked up over the next few days, by walking and then running around it. I was, after all, supposed to be getting into shape; chugging along the beach seemed as good a way as any.

The sand was solid and smooth down below the high-tide mark. The tides didn't seem to be very pronounced in the bay, but there was enough rise to give me a good clear path all around the island if I timed it right. If I didn't, as I found out the first day, I wound up slogging back to the trailer in soft, foot-dragging dry sand, cursing and sweating.

Now and then, just for variety, I wandered up into the dunes and had a look around. There wasn't much to see, just more dunes and more grass waving in the wind—the wind blew all the time; after hardly any time you quit noticing it, but it was always there, whining in your ears and blowing sand into everything—and a few small pools of rainwater that were alive with the most murderous mosquitoes I'd ever come across. About midway down the island, near the narrow part, somebody had put up some wooden benches and a couple of picnic tables in the shade of a bunch of live-oaks. The first few morning runs, I was damn glad of something to sit down on.

Sit down hell, collapse. I was in worse shape than I'd let myself believe. The first time I tried to run any distance at all, my lungs filled with what felt like bursting napalm and my heart pounded like a runaway diesel engine. I wobbled back to the trailer on wet-noodle legs that seemed to belong to someone else, telling myself I was going to have to get serious about this.

I mean, I'd never been the jock type; even as a kid I hated to run any distance—which was why I went out for wrestling in high school instead of football—and one of the things I really loathed about Fort Benning was that endless damn double-timing everywhere you went, with some asshole with three stripes yelling at you to move like you got a purpose. I'd always made it a rule, when some otherwise rational-looking guy started to tell me how many miles he ran each morning, to get up and make an excuse to move farther down the bar . . . and once I broke off a promising affair with a really amazingly-constructed Danish girl because she wouldn't quit waking me up at five in the morning insisting I run a few miles with her. Runners. . . .

But, like it or not, there were times in my line of work when you had to run like hell—usually with no prior notice and no time for stretching exercises or psyching up, either, and often as not without even a chance to put your clothes on. I reminded myself, as I set out on the next painful lope down the beach, of what would have happened to me on several occasions in the past if I'd run a little slower.

And when the firestorm began in my lungs and my legs started sending up messages that they wouldn't be responsible if I kept this nonsense up any longer, I replayed a few mental pictures of what had happened to people I'd known who hadn't run fast enough, or had stopped running too soon. The sight of Mattson's body, still tied to that tree, after the Angolans and their Cuban "advisors" had finished with him; or trying to find enough of Walters to turn over to Graves Registration when the mortar barrage finally lifted . . . somehow I found I could still run a little longer and a little faster. The weekend-marathon crowd ought to look into the idea.

Gradually the morning workouts began to take effect. The pain didn't go away, but it became something I could live with, and my vision no longer blurred and the Karankawa war drums quit sounding in my head. The long-legged sea birds on the beach began to get used to me, and no longer flew away, but simply stalked aside and watched me jog past, no doubt thinking that it took all kinds. I could feel my muscles firming up under the sunburned skin and the accumulated toxins of the Third World pumping out through my pores. And before too many days I was able to run clear around the island—not very fast yet, and still having to stop and blow a few times, but it was a start. I finished up with a quick dip in the little cove by the house, and later I started adding a long afternoon swim. One of the books had mentioned that there were sharks in the vicinity, but nothing ate me.

And I slept nights now, and there were no more dreams.

I was getting ready to go for my afternoon swim, in fact, the day I finally had company on the island. I was sitting on the sand, just about to take off my sneakers, when I heard the sound from somewhere down the beach: the deep, slightly nasal roar of a big outboard motor throttling down from wide-open to just above idle. Somebody, obviously, was approaching the island, coming close inshore from the sound of it; maybe just a fisherman or a curious tourist, maybe not.

I got up and climbed up to the house, but even from the deck I couldn't see anything: whoever it was was hidden by the dunes and the live-oaks. I stood there a few minutes, wondering whether I ought to go check it out. There was no reason to believe anyone was coming ashore, and it was pretty hot to go chasing off down the beach again; I still wasn't up to a second run in a day.

But then I began hearing other sounds: loud, unintelligible shouts, male voices, several of them. They sounded high-spirited rather than angry or distressed. I remembered what Cameron had said about kids coming out from the mainland. The outboard's drone suddenly stopped. There were several faint thumps and clangs and splashes.

I sighed to myself; time, it would seem, for Dane to start earning his keep around here. I wished they'd picked a cooler day. The Gulf sun was up and the breeze only seemed to push the hot air around. Even the seagulls looked as if they were wishing they had a few cold beers.

I don't really know why I went by the trailer and picked up the shotgun. Being cautious, maybe, though I still wasn't taking the situation all that seriously. In fact, by the time I was halfway down the beach, I was beginning to feel acutely embarrassed to be holding the damn thing; if there'd been any place I could have set it down without getting it full of sand, I probably would have left it.

I trotted along, sneakers crunching in the damp sand, holding the shotgun in a kind of Port Arms position—I had a momentary impulse to begin singing "I Wanta Be an Airborne Ranger," though I managed to resist it—and hearing the shouts and whoops coming with undiminished enthusiasm across the dunes. I knew where they were, now; they had to be down by the narrow part of the island, where there was a good-sized cove and the best stretch of beach on the island. Now I began to hear the cracking and splintering sounds of wood being broken up. Another motor started up, this one high-pitched and tinny: a chainsaw, for God's sake.

That was when I stopped and racked a round into the chamber of the shotgun. After all, this *was* Texas, and I saw that movie too. . . .

I left the beach and went up through the dunes, coming down on the visitors through the live-oaks, so I could see them before they saw me. It was pretty much as I'd expected.

There were six of them: suntanned, husky-looking young louts, somewhere between eighteen and twenty-five by the look of them, all of them barefoot and wearing faded shorts, a couple in T-shirts and the others bareback, all but one wearing mesh-back gimme caps. Their boat, a big, fast-looking fiberglass job—I didn't know the make—was nosed up to the beach, with one kid tying its bow line to a big piece of driftwood. Already the beach was littered with folding chairs, plastic ice chests, loose cartons and single cans of beer. As I came in sight, the bareheaded kid finished a beer and tossed the can onto the sand.

Up under the trees, the one with the chainsaw was busy cutting up one of the picnic tables, the little motor whining and complaining as he pushed the teeth through the heavy redwood planks. Two of his buddies were already carrying pieces of wood down to the beach, where there seemed to be plans to build a fire.

There was no need to try to move silently; even if the chainsaw hadn't been screaming away like a mutant dentist's drill, they were all yelling and cursing at the tops of their lungs for no apparent reason beyond sheer mindless exuberance. I could have ridden up on a brontosaurus and they wouldn't have noticed.

I watched them for a moment. Then I stepped out from under the trees into the sunlight and said, "Hey."

They didn't hear me, of course, but the ones on the beach saw me, and a minute later the others did too. The one with the chainsaw shut it down and came walking slowly down the side of the dune toward me. All of them were silent, staring at me. Evidently it was my move.

I said, "Private island, guys. Have to take your party somewhere else."

I would have added "Sorry," if they hadn't demolished the bench I sat down on to rest during my workouts. I was going to miss that bench, damn it.

The one near the boat, a tall skinny redhead, started to say something. I said, "Not open for discussion, kid. Load up and move out."

The chainsaw artist spat on the sand. He was a big blond with punk-mean eyes and what looked like a pretty bad overbite. He had on a ripped yellow T-shirt that said PARTY NAKED. It was obvious he was the leader of this particular pack; you could find him in any poolroom, or sitting on a fender on any high-school parking lot, or in any city jail, anywhere in the United States. Or in any infantry squad, where his kind did become valuable persons: you could send them down a trail first and see if anybody shot at them before you risked the more intelligent troops.

I realized suddenly that he was about to ask me if I thought I was big enough to make them.

He said, "You think you're big enough to make us?"

I'd been holding the shotgun down alongside my leg, not out of sight but inconspicuous. I raised it now, holding it across my chest, not pointing it at anyone or anything, just letting them see it.

I said, "I don't know, son. This is how big I am. How big are you?"

There was a general intake of breath and some muttering and muffled cursing, none of the words very original. A couple of them began edging toward the boat. They all seemed to be looking at PARTY NAKED more than at me, waiting to see what he would do.

If he'd been alone, he probably wouldn't have pushed it. But his status as King Rat in these parts was on the line. He'd laid down a challenge and been answered, and the rules of his world—as rigid and elaborate in their own pathetic way as anything the samurai ever devised—said that he had to go on with the dance.

He said, "You ain't going to use that." A kind of cocky smirk came out and planted itself on the corners of his mouth. "No way."

Christ, I wanted to tell him, get out of here, kid, you have no idea what you're dealing with here, I was killing better men than you before you were born—and the rest of you, what kind of pitiful geeks are you to let this jackoff lead you?

Then I remembered that the shotgun only held a few rounds of nearly harmless skeet shot that wouldn't stop traffic on a dead-end street; and suddenly PARTY NAKED's chances looked a good deal better.

He said slowly, "I think we're just gonna—"

I didn't wait to find out what he thought they were just gonna. I snapped the shotgun's muzzle down and fired. A fountain of flying sand suddenly obscured the nearest twelve-pack. When the sand blew away there was a heap of riddled cans and a puddle of cheap beer soaking slowly into the beach.

Somebody said, "Holy fuckin' shit!"

They all stared at the ruined twelve-pack. It looked pretty impressive. The shredded cardboard hid the tininess of the holes in the cans. The bareheaded boy said mournfully, "Aw, look, what'd you go do *that* for. . . ."

I said, "Okay, enough bullshit. Let's go."

I think they'd have gone, but then the redhead suddenly snickered and said, "Looks like he's big enough, Ray."

And PARTY NAKED came unglued, charging straight at me across the sand, fists doubled, head down, making a kind of strange whining sob in his throat: pure redneck kamikaze, and me with a practically unloaded gun.

I might have been able to take him fair and I might not. I'd had training he couldn't even conceive of, but on the other hand I was still out of shape and he was big and young and, at the moment, half-drunk and crazy. I didn't bother finding out. I dropped into a crouch as he came in and rammed the shotgun's muzzle into his gut, just below the breastbone, the blunt barrel sinking in better than an inch. He said, "*Unh*," and I yanked the shotgun back, swung it up over my left shoulder, and slammed the buttplate home between his eyes, which now held a look of intense amazement. It was the old classic bayonet routine, thrust-and-buttstroke, and if I'd put my full weight into it I'd have killed him as surely as if I'd had a real bayonet. As it was he merely rolled his eyes back, turned a strange color, and fell slowly onto the sand. As a kind of afterthought I kicked him in the crotch on his way down.

The others stood frozen, staring huge-eyed like a tree full of owls. I racked the shotgun's action and blasted another twelve-pack into oblivion. They all jumped.

I said, "Pick him up and get your stuff and get out of here. Now."

They moved, after a second, scattering out across the beach to pick up their stuff, a couple of them hoisting the unconscious Ray between them and half-dragging him toward the boat. I thought about making them leave the beer, but it wasn't my brand and I'd have had to carry it back to the trailer. None of them spoke, to me or to each other.

The redhead went up to the picnic area and got the chainsaw. I waited until he came back across the beach and I said, "Hey. Bring that thing here."

He hesitated. I gestured with the shotgun and he nodded quickly and trotted over toward me, carrying the chainsaw.

I gestured again and he set it down on the sand and backed away.

I watched as they loaded the last of their junk onto the boat. I should have made them clean up their litter, but by now I wanted to be rid of them. As they started the motor and backed slowly out into the cove, I bent down and picked up the chainsaw. It wasn't very big and it didn't seem to be a very high-quality one.

With their eyes following me, I waded out into the cove until the water was nearly up to my waist, holding the shotgun in one hand and the chainsaw in the other; then, deliberately and looking straight at them, I dropped the chainsaw into the water, turned my back on them, and sloshed back toward the beach. By the time I reached the shore, they had the boat up at wide-open throttle and were moving fast toward the distant line of the mainland, the hull bouncing and banging in the afternoon chop.

I looked at the scatter of empty cans and cardboard boxes and splintered planks and considered cleaning things up, but it was too hot and there was no urgency about it. Let it wait till morning; I wanted a beer or two of my own. I cleared the shotgun's chamber, fed the round back into the tubular magazine, and was about to move out homeward when I realized that there was a man standing in the shadow of the nearest live-oak, watching me, not moving.

Before I could get my mind unstuck, a soft low chuckle drifted out from the shadows, quiet and wispy as a wasp's feet on a window. A dry high-pitched voice said, "Handled them pretty good, didn't you?"

I didn't exactly jump, but I came close. While I stood there staring and, probably, looking as stupid as the kids had looked a moment ago, he chuckled again and stepped out into the sunlight: a little old man, not much over five feet tall and skinny as a crane, dressed in white-faded jeans and a ragged-brimmed straw hat. That was it, no shirt, no shoes; well, he wasn't trying to get served at McDonald's. His skin was a dark reddish-brown color, the shade of rust on an old exhaust manifold. His face, as best I could see it under his hat brim, was lined like a map of the Mekong Delta. He cocked his head back to look up at me and I saw a pair of dark, Oriental-looking eyes that seemed to be enjoying a private joke.

"Hello," he said with a big grin that didn't seem to contain any teeth. "My name's Billy Jumper. I run the boat dock over at Bayport."

I remembered now; I'd only seen him briefly, and not close up, the day Cameron had brought me out to the island. I hadn't heard his name before, hadn't really thought about him at all.

He said, "Sorry to come up on you like that. My motor cut out on me, over on the other side of the island. I was gonna walk down to your place when I heard those boys with their boat over here."

I said, "How long have you been standing there?"

He tilted his head to one side, making him look more than ever like some kind of bird. "Since just before you showed up."

That meant I'd walked right past him, damn near close enough to touch him, and hadn't known he was there. Christ.

He said, "Wonder if I could borrow a few tools from you, see if I can get that motor fixed enough to get home. It's a long paddle back across the channel."

His voice held a slight accent; or maybe not so much a true accent as just a difference in cadence, a little hesitancy in phrasing. It was the speech of a man who spoke English perfectly well but was used to thinking in some other language. I couldn't pin it down, though. He looked almost

Vietnamese, but not quite. Mexican, maybe?

"Seminole," he said, though I hadn't asked. "Knew you were gonna ask, people always do. Save you working up to it."

"Seminole?" I wondered why I hadn't realized he was an Indian. He could have posed for an old nickel, if he'd had braids. "I didn't know there were any Seminoles in this area."

"There's not, except for me. I just settled here about twenty years back, when I retired. Preached for a lot of years," he said with another toothless grin. "Finally just got too old to handle all the crap, maybe got too ugly for them to look at, so I came down here and took over that old boat dock. Pays about as good as the church ever did, you get right down to it."

"You came here from Florida?"

"Oklahoma. More Seminoles there than there are in Florida, now. Been separated so long we can't talk the language with them any more—get together with a Florida Seminole, we have to talk English." He cleared his throat. "About those tools—"

I said, "I don't really know if I've got what you'd need, tell the truth. I've never had occasion to check out the tool situation here . . . look," I said after thinking for a second, "why don't I just run you over to your place and let you get whatever you need? Or maybe I could give you a tow so you wouldn't have to come back."

He was nodding. "Sure, sure, if you don't mind doing that. I got a rope. Be a lot easier for me that way."

I gestured up the beach. "I'll have to go up there and get my boat. You want to wait here, let me pick you up?"

"Oh, no, that's all right, I'll walk with you." He stuck out his hand. "I didn't catch your name," he said politely.

"Dane." I took his hand, remembering just in time what a Mohawk sergeant had told me long ago: Indians don't like bruiser handshakes, which they regard as rude and even possibly hostile. His grip was soft but I could feel surprising strength in the thin old hand.

He said, "Dane, Dane. You're not from around here, are you?"

"No. From Kentucky, originally. I haven't been home in a long time." God, was that ever true. "There's supposedly some Shawnee blood in our family," I added, "but I don't really know anything about it." I stopped, feeling stupid again. "Hell, you must get so damn tired of white people telling you they're part Indian."

He laughed out loud this time. "Oh, I don't know. When I was a boy, a white man would shoot you if you said he had Indian blood. Maybe it's a little bit of a step up."

We walked along the beach toward the house. He moved well on the hard damp sand, his bare feet making no sound. I didn't have to go slow for him and I had a feeling he could have kept up if I'd broken into a run. I said, "If you've been here that long you must have retired young."

He glanced sideways at me, his eyes doing their private-joke twinkle. "Son, I'll be eighty years old next year."

"Son of a bitch."

"So I been told," he said with a straight face. "Say," he said, "good job on those boys back there. I know some of the families, most of them are just wild kids with nothing much to do, but that Ray's a mean one. Him and his daddy, they're in that Ku Klux Klan, couple of times they tried to run me off, threatened to burn my place. I got a kick out of what you did."

I said, "Nice talk from a preacher."

"Hell, son, I told you, I'm retired. I can speak my mind nowadays." He spat expressively on the sand.

"The Cherokees got a saying about people like that.
They say God ought to send them someplace where
the bottles all have holes in them and the women
don't."

We rigged a tow line from my boat to his and cruised
slowly across the channel to the mainland. I was keeping an
eye open for the kids with their big powerboat—they could
have swamped or rammed us easily if they'd been in the
area and feeling vengeful—but there was no sign of them.
I kept the speed down so as not to bounce Billy Jumper
around too much. When I looked back he was sitting calmly
in the stern of his battered old aluminum skiff, puffing at a
stubby-stemmed pipe, apparently enjoying the ride. As we
used to say, he was so cool you could have chilled beer
up his ass.

When we got to the dock and tied the boats up I helped
him unship the conked-out outboard and lug it up to his
shed. "Thanks a lot," he said. "Wait just a minute."

He went back to his boat and came back holding a
stringer of some sort of good-sized fish. I didn't know
what they were; sea fishing was never one of my sports.

"Here," he said. "Ought to get yourself a few bites out
of these here. Imagine you work up a pretty good appetite
running up and down like that. Oh, yeah," he grinned, "I
see you all the time while I'm out fishing. You in training
for something?"

"No. I've been . . . sick," I said. "Sort of. Trying to get
back in shape."

"Huh." He peered closely at me. "Wait here another
minute."

He disappeared into the shed and returned, after a long
minute, with a small plastic bag. It appeared to contain
some dried leaves and twigs, and some bits of evergreen.

"Burn this," he said, "where you sleep. Stand in the smoke and breathe it in. Don't worry, it's not funny stuff, nothing against the law. Just Indian medicine."

A big, scruffy-looking old cat came up and jumped up onto a nearby gasoline drum. He was a yellowish tabby and visibly hung like a porno actor. I scratched him behind the ears and he made a purr that almost shook the dock. Billy Jumper said, "That old tomcat's been hanging around here almost a year. Never saw him take up with anybody like that before. You like cats?"

I shrugged. "Sometimes. The ones like this, not the shaggy-assed house pets. I like the kind that go their own way."

The old man looked me up and down. "I believe that," he said slowly. "I think you would . . . well. Thanks for the help." He stuck out his hand again. "Come see me if you need anything."

I didn't see the kids in the powerboat on the way back, either, but I held the throttle open all the way. When I got back to the island and started to tie the skiff up at the little dock, I saw a ragged-eared head poke up from behind the clutter of ropes and gas cans in the bow. There was a brief sound like a rusty nail being pulled out of a very old board.

I said, "Well, I'll be damned."

The tomcat jumped up onto the dock, as if he'd been living here all his life, and jerked his tail a couple of times in a satisfied sort of way. I said, "Make yourself at home, I guess. What's your name?"

He looked at me and said, "*Rrrowl.*"

"Raoul?" He did look a little like a Raoul I used to know, a big, mean-tempered ex-Legionnaire I'd worked with briefly, never mind where. At least the facial expression and general attitude were much the same, and I figured their sex lives were probably similar too. "Okay, Raoul. Get your ass out of the way and I'll see what we can do with these fish."

That evening, about an hour after sunset, I was sitting in a folding chair in front of the trailer, digesting Billy Jumper's fish and watching Raoul pick at the leftovers. Inside, the radio was playing a new song by somebody named Dwight Yoakum. I'd never heard of him before but he was damn good, a lot like the early Hank Williams. I was feeling pretty good, all in all. The only thing that spoiled the evening was the constant attacks of squadrons of giant mosquitoes. They could have made a movie about Gulf Coast mosquitoes and called it "Beaks" . . . they were enormous and hungry and they didn't scare for shit.

Finally I decided the light above the trailer door would have to go. I didn't need it on a clear night like this anyway. I got up and started toward the trailer to switch it off.

Just then I became aware of a steady droning sound, getting rapidly louder, from somewhere out in the channel between my island and the barrier islands. It was a sound I'd heard before, and not all that long ago.

I knew suddenly what was going to happen. I lunged toward the dangling light-switch string, but then something whacked sharply into the trailer's metal side and I dropped flat on the sand as the first sharp *bang* came across the water.

There were three shots in rapid succession, all of them hitting the trailer pretty high up, then a pause, then two more lower down. They seemed to be aiming at the light, or at least using it as an aiming point. I looked up cautiously and saw the reddish-orange flashes of two more shots, well out on the water.

There was no real danger at that range and with the evening chop rocking the boat, but I stayed down just in case my statistical luck was off. There were no more shots, though. A high crazy yell drifted down the wind and then the engine note was rising again as the shooters headed for the inshore channel, moving fast. Not a very determined attack, but then they didn't know what sort of armament I might have on hand. It had probably taken them all evening, and a lot of cheap booze, to work themselves up this much. I wondered if it had been Ray himself doing the shooting, or one of his tickbirds. He probably wouldn't want to delegate an honor like that.

I got up and knocked the sand off my clothes. Raoul was nowhere to be seen; that cat was no fool. The trailer didn't seem to have sustained any damage beyond a few holes that would be easily patched. The radio was still playing.

I fingered one of the holes. Thirty caliber, it looked like. From the sound of the shots I guessed the weapon had been one of those .30-30 lever-action carbines, probably the most popular and common rifle, other than .22s, in the state of Texas. Maybe in the United States, for all I knew. Not much gun by the standards I was used to, perhaps—in Lebanon you couldn't have given one away—but perfectly capable of tearing a man's head off.

The boat's engine noise died away up the channel to the north. It was quiet again except for the radio and the muffled burr of the generator engine over in the concrete blockhouse, and the whine of another batch of mosquitoes. I stared at the holes, thinking.

Next morning when I tied up at the boat dock Billy Jumper was standing up on the dock waiting for me. "Saw you coming," he said. "Did I hear some shooting out your way last night? You all right?"

I nodded. "Listen," I said, "do you own a gun you'd like to sell?"

He shook his head. "Don't own a gun at all. Haven't since the big war."

"Well," I said, "is there any place around here where they sell guns and ammunition?"

He took off his straw hat and scratched his head. His hair was white and thick. "There's a gun shop up in Soto."

"Would you drive me there?"

"Sure," he said.

4

• • • • •

SOTO WAS A DUSTY, BURNED-OUT-LOOKING LIT-
tle place surrounded by miles of dead-flat coastal plain. It
didn't seem to have any real reason for being there. Its
three-block "business district" was nearly deserted. Even
the Baptist church needed paint and a new roof. In Texas
that's a very bad sign.

One thing, though, they had a hell of a gun shop in
Soto. You could have staged a coup in a small country
with less firepower than they had in that shop. In fact I've
seen it done.

The guy behind the counter said, "Something for home
protection, and you say you're living on an island? Did you
have in mind a pistol or a long gun?"

He was a thin, pale, gray-haired man with heavy rimless
glasses and a sort of scholarly style about him; he looked
and sounded like a professor at some minor college, maybe
a Presbyterian seminary. Certainly he wasn't much like the
burr-head, no-neck, borderline-psycho stereotype of the
Texas gun dealer, as depicted in movies and TV and
magazines by liberal types who don't think they engage in
stereotyping. He didn't even have a Marine Corps tattoo.

I said, "Both, I guess. I don't really know what sort
of situation I may have to deal with." If at all; chances
were that Ray and his buddies, having made a face-saving

attack last night, would drop the whole thing and take their antisocial business elsewhere. But I wasn't going to gamble on it, and I was definitely through relying on birdshot and bluff.

He nodded crisply and led the way toward the rear of the store. "Well, here are a few rifles you might find suitable—"

I looked at a few used and new military semi-automatics— what the media, with their usual gift for getting everything wrong, like to call "assault rifles"—but the prices were high and I didn't really see any point in the things; most such weapons are clumsy if you're not going to be firing them full-auto. Instead I settled on a Remington semi-auto hunting rifle in .30-06 with a 2X Weaver scope, used but clean. It held a mere eight shots but I figured if I couldn't do the job with that I probably couldn't do it at all. I had the man get me a few boxes of 180-grain soft-nosed cartridges and then we went over to look at the pistols.

I knew what I wanted there; after more than three quarters of a century, they still haven't improved, in my view, on the old Government Model .45 automatic. It will go on shooting when the fancier pieces clog up with mud and sand: it handles and points well if you have big hands, which I have, and people you shoot with it tend to stay shot. And if all else fails it makes a great club.

I wasn't prepared for the prices, though. Short guns seemed to have gone through the ozone layer since the last time I'd bought one in the United States—whenever that had been; I realized suddenly that I couldn't remember. And it was obvious that the .45 auto, even old Army-surplus pieces, had become one of the hotter items on the market. I had a fair amount of money at the moment, and more in several banks in New York and a number of foreign cities, but this was ridiculous. I picked out an old but solid Smith

& Wesson .38 instead and said the hell with it. The man produced some nasty-looking hollow-point loads that he said would considerably make up for the deficiencies of the smaller caliber.

When we had everything piled on the counter and my mind had begun to recover a little from the shock of finding out how much all this was going to cost—for a second I wondered if it might be cheaper just to pay any intruder to go away—the man took out a clipboard with some legal-looking forms and said, "All right, sir, now to begin with I've got to see proof of Texas residence."

I stopped, hand on wallet. "What?"

"It's the law, sir. Federal Firearms Act. Surely you knew?"

I shook my head. "I've been out of the country awhile."

"I can't sell you any guns," he said, looking pissed off and slapping the forms with the back of his hand, "without filling out these chickenshit things." The word seemed so out of character I almost did a double take. "One of the requirements is that you must be a resident of the state where you buy the weapon. I have to see a Texas driver's license or equivalent identification."

He frowned suddenly, peering at me over his glasses. "Ah, you *do* have . . . ?"

Well, hell. I should have known, should have asked before I wasted his time and mine. Of course you don't expect that kind of thing in Texas, but I knew the Federal people had been increasingly tiresome on the subject of firearms in the last decade or so—even I wasn't that out of touch.

I said, "I'm sorry. I'm not even sure I'm a legal resident of *any* state right now."

I'd have had trouble even proving I was an American citizen at the moment. My passport, along with most of

my other papers, remained somewhere in Africa. I had
a Virginia driver's license, thanks to a bit of low-level
Company string-pulling, but that was all. I didn't even
have a valid credit card.

He sighed. "I'm sorry too. I should have told you in
the beginning. I wish I could help you," he said. "After
all, like any other businessman, I want to sell my goods.
But the law is very strict. . . . The idea," he said, "is, supposedly, to keep residents of states with strict anti-gun
laws, such as New York, from going into neighboring
states with less restrictive ordinances and arming themselves."

"Shit."

"My sentiments exactly." He tossed the clipboard onto
a shelf below the cash register. "Of course in those same
states any street criminal knows a dozen or more sources
from which he can purchase anything up to and including
the latest submachine guns, but at least we've seen to it that
the ordinary citizen isn't going to be able to shoot back.
I'm not much interested in politics," he said, "but when any
government no longer trusts its own citizens with arms, I
put it to you that that government itself is no longer to be
trusted."

I didn't feel like getting into an argument. Anyway, I
agreed with him. I said, "Well. I don't suppose you know
any, uh, private citizens around here who might have something to sell?"

"If I had a day or two to ask around, I might find you
something. I had the impression you were in a bit more of
a hurry?"

"Yes."

"Hm. Now I *can* help you in one area. You said you've
got a shotgun? What caliber?"

"Twenty-gauge."

"Right. Here we are." He took a couple of yellow-and-green boxes from under the counter and set them in front of me. "Buckshot doesn't work very well in anything smaller than twelve-gauge, I'm afraid, but these Number Fours will be lethal against a human target at close range." He might have been a druggist recommending a headache remedy. "Say out to forty or fifty feet, though I wouldn't rely on them beyond half that range if I had a choice. These," he said, tapping the other box, "are slugs, solid lead shot. Not very accurate compared to a rifle, but capable of killing a man out to as much as a hundred yards."

"Or sinking a boat?"

"Why, yes, I'd think so. If you hit it enough times in the right places, I don't know why not. Though I've never heard of anyone trying it."

Well, it was better than what I had, that was certain. At night the shotgun might even be better than a rifle. I started to pick up the boxes. "You can sell me these?"

"Oh, to be sure. Just another idiotic quirk in the law—I can sell you any quantity of shotgun ammunition, including buckshot and slugs, without any identification whatever. You could be a raving narcotics addict or an Arab terrorist in full uniform, wouldn't matter. On the other hand I can't sell you a single cartridge for a .22 target pistol. Now let me show you something else."

He went back to the pistol case. "If you genuinely need something for personal protection. . . ."

He handed me a big, heavy, old-fashioned-looking revolver. It looked like the sort of thing you'd see in a museum or a Civil War book.

"Cap-and-ball revolver," he explained. "Not an antique, but a modern replica of the 1860 Colt Army .44—what people sometimes call a 'Dragoon pistol.' Very popular," he added as I studied the gun, "with enthusiasts who like to shoot historic weapons but don't want to risk damage to a valuable antique. They're also used quite a bit in the movies, or in re-enactments of Civil War battles and the like."

It wasn't as clumsy as it looked; actually the old-fashioned piece had a nice balance and seemed to point naturally. The hole in the muzzle suggested it would make a satisfactory impact on anything, or anyone, you shot with it.

"The point is," he said, "these are not covered by existing laws. They aren't even legally considered firearms. I can sell you one with no problems at all."

The idea did have a certain appeal; at least it would give me a backup weapon to go with the shotgun. And, after all, a lot of men had been killed with guns of this sort: Yanks and Rebs, outlaws and rustlers and marshals, to say nothing of Billy Jumper's relatives and other Indians. None of whom, from all I'd heard, had been exactly pushovers.

"Here," the gray-haired man said, holding out another revolver, "we have what they call the Sheriff's Model—same gun with a four-inch barrel. If you expect to need to conceal it—"

"No." I wouldn't have any need for a concealed weapon until I went back to work—if then—and when that time came, I'd get it from sources that didn't have to fill out Federal forms. Out on the island, if I did have to use a one-hand gun at all, I'd probably be glad of the extra power and accuracy of the longer barrel. "This one will be fine," I said. "Can you show me how to load it?"

The gun came with a little instruction leaflet, but he took me through the drill just the same: a complicated and slow business involving loose black powder, cast lead balls, and copper percussion caps. It was clear that six shots would be all I could count on when the balloon went up; reloading one of these things under fire just wasn't a reasonable proposition. No wonder the old-timers carried two.

"One thing," he said as he rang up the total. "This black powder here is extremely explosive, much touchier than modern smokeless ammunition. I strongly advise you to keep it stored well away from flame or heat—though in a dry place; it will absorb water right out of the air—and, if possible, away from your house."

I said, "Thanks for all the help."

"Oh, don't mention it." He gave me a tight little smile. "I enjoy finding ways to circumvent stupid laws. The American way, right?"

Back on the island, that afternoon, I took the guns down to the southern end and tried them out. It didn't take much experimentation to determine that the shotgun was capable of doing some very ugly things at close range with the Number Fours and that the big lead slugs would make a hell of a hole in anything they hit, but anyone at any real distance was going to have to be very unlucky to get hit by either load.

The .44 was something else. It made an amazingly loud *boom*, not at all like a modern big-bore pistol, and punched impressive holes, yet the recoil wasn't nearly as severe as you'd have thought. Given the incredibly crude sights—a little brass bead at the muzzle and a notch filed into the tip of the hammer—it seemed to be fairly accurate; on the whole it compared reasonably well, shot for shot, with a GI .45.

It also made more smoke than I'd have thought possible. Movies be damned, the marshal and the bad guys never shot it out in the saloon with these things—or if they did they were groping around shooting by feel after the first few shots.

And reloading, my God! It was even worse than it had sounded in the shop at Soto. Measure out a charge of black powder with the little brass dipper. Ram a soft-lead ball down on top of the powder, using the funny-looking lever under the barrel; if you did it right, there would be a little round lead shaving left. Fit a percussion cap to the nipple at the rear of the cylinder, being careful not to blow your fingers off. Seal the whole works with a dollop of the special grease from the little can. Do this six times and you were ready to go. Of course, by this time anyone you intended to shoot would have hauled ass or killed you, but that was how you did it anyway. And, I reminded myself, plenty of people *had* done it, often with bullets and arrows zipping past their noses. My respect for the old-timers rose considerably.

I set up some improvised targets, mostly empty beer cans left by Ray's little beach party, and boomed away until I found out where the .44 shot. It turned out that simply pointing the piece by instinct worked better than trying to use the primitive sights. Since I didn't have a holster—I hadn't seen any need for one in the present circumstances—I didn't bother practicing any fast-response routines.

When I was satisfied, I lugged everything back down the beach to the trailer and began the chore of cleaning the .44. The man in Soto had been very explicit on the need for cleaning thoroughly after every use; apparently black-powder residue combined rapidly with the moist and salty air to lunch any untended weapon. The cleaning routine was a tiresome and messy one, involving complete disassembly and a lot of solvent and hot water. Before I was done I was wishing I'd waited until the cool of the evening.

When I had everything back together and the cylinder reloaded and capped, I looked around for a safe place to stash the can of black powder. There was only one logical choice. I got out my ring of keys and walked back to the concrete blockhouse.

I'd been in and out of the generator room God knew how many times, refueling and otherwise fiddling with the generator engine, but I hadn't even looked inside the main storage room. I looked around with some interest, remembering the purpose for which it had been built. There was nothing at all to recall the fortunes in illegal drugs that the ugly low-ceilinged room must once have contained. There were only such mundane odds and ends as a rusting, partly disassembled bicycle—somebody must have gone in for riding along the beach—and a lot of tools piled and tumbled on the rough board shelves along the walls.

I put the can of black powder on a shelf in the far corner and set the little box of percussion caps beside it. There was no point in keeping any of the stuff nearer to hand. If I used up all six loads in the gun without resolving matters, and couldn't switch to the shotgun for some reason, I wasn't going to get that thing stoked again fast enough to help. There wasn't any good reason for keeping the powder and caps at all, except that I'd paid for them.

As I left the blockhouse and locked up, the sound of a motor came drifting across the channel. It sounded considerably smaller than Ray's big powerboat, and when I looked I thought there was something familiar about the distant shape headed my way. Sure enough, it was Billy Jumper.

I went down to the dock and waited for him. He pulled in and cut his motor but he didn't move to come ashore. He just sat there in his boat, grinning up at me. "Heard some shooting," he said. "That you trying out your new gun?"

I nodded. He said, "Figured. I guess I should have come out to check, but I didn't see any boats around. Anyway, I don't know that I'd have done you any good. Like I said, I don't even own a gun."

He got out his pipe and looked at it and then put it back in his pocket. "Look," he said, "you got any plans for this evening?"

I looked around at the dunes and the dock and the waving grass. "As you can imagine," I said, "I've got a hell of a social schedule out here. Having Charles and Di and the gang out for champagne, then I thought I'd run my yacht over to Bayport and take in the opera."

He was chuckling his dry little chuckle. "Figured that too. What I had in mind," he said, "if you can get loose from the rich and famous, is there's something I wanted to show you. Thought you might find it interesting."

He didn't explain further. It didn't matter; I didn't have anything else to do. I said, "Sure."

"Come over around sundown," he said. "Meet you at the dock. We got to wait till after dark anyway. Oh, and wear some shoes or boots you can walk in, and some long pants," he added, reaching for his motor. "We got to do a little bushwhacking."

Just before sunset I opened a can of tuna for Raoul—there was a whole case of it in the trailer and I hated the stuff—and locked up and headed across the channel to Bayport. Billy Jumper was waiting in his old pickup truck. I'd always heard Indians were hopelessly unpunctual but he didn't seem to know about it. I climbed in beside him and he said, "Evening," and started the engine. The truck was at least twenty years old and there was hardly a square inch that didn't have a dent or a rust patch, but the engine ran quietly and smoothly. He drove out along the blacktop for a couple of miles and turned up an unmarked dirt road. "Got a ways to go," he said.

He glanced sideways at me. "What I said earlier," he said, "about not having a gun. I wasn't trying to be holier-than-thou about it or anything. Hope you didn't think I was, what do the kids say, putting you down."

I said, "No problem."

"Huh. See these people all the time now, running around wanting you to know they don't smoke, don't drink, don't eat meat, don't shoot guns, don't do this and don't do that. It's a damn poor man that defines himself by the things he doesn't do." He chuckled. "If I was still in the business I could get me a pretty good sermon out of that, you know?"

He swerved to miss a suicidal armadillo. "I was at Anzio," he said. "And a bunch of other fights after that. Killed a lot of Germans and Italians, they even gave me a couple of medals. After it was all over, though, I swore I'd never pick up a gun again. That's when I took up preaching. Some of these amateur headshrinkers might say I was trying to make up for something. Who knows, they might even be right."

The old pickup hit a hole and bounced so hard my ass came off the seat. Billy Jumper said something under his breath in what I assumed must be Seminole. "I still do a little hunting," he said, "but only with a bow and arrow. Make my own tackle and so on, guess I'm one of the few Indians left doing it the old way. Just kind of a hobby, and I don't do as much of that as I used to."

He laughed. "Boy, some of my ancestors would be shocked to hear how I turned out. Did you know the Seminole War was the longest war the U.S. Army ever fought? Went on longer than Viet Nam and involved a bigger percentage of the standing Army than any other war in history. Congress had to enlarge the size of the Army to keep up with the drain. We were one mean bunch of Indians in the old days. Guess I'm letting the tradition down."

I said suddenly, "I killed a blind man once."

I don't know what the hell made me tell him that; it just came out, and when I heard myself saying it I couldn't believe it. I wouldn't have been much more shocked to find myself turning into a werewolf. I suppose it was just the effect Billy Jumper had on me. Somehow it seemed that you could tell the old man anything at all and know that it would never go any further. I didn't know what church he had worked for, but he'd have made a hell of a great priest.

He said after a moment, "Well, you know, these things happen. I remember in Italy—"

"It wasn't in a war." Now it was coming out, might as well tell it all. "At least it wasn't my country's war, and I wasn't in uniform. I shot him from ambush," I said. "He was a Muslim holy man, a mullah, and he was on his way to lead prayers at the mosque, and he was stone blind, and I shot him down in his own doorway. He was the leader of a bunch of extremists," I went on, "and he was behind a lot of serious terrorism and the deaths of a good many innocent people—including children—but that wasn't why I killed him."

Billy Jumper said quietly, "Were you with the CIA or something?"

"Not at the time. I did it for money," I said. "It wasn't even the United States that paid me. I was working for some other Arabs, high-level Saudis who were afraid his sect would spread to their country and threaten their control. The CIA knew about it, but I was strictly free-lancing."

I didn't even try to hold back now. Maybe it was time it all spilled out. Who cared any more, anyway?

"I did it because they offered me a great deal of money," I said. "My wife was in a hospital in Switzerland and they said she needed an operation that was going to cost more than I had. Right then I'd have shot the Pope to save her."

He said, "Did it?"

"Hell, no. You're way ahead of me, aren't you? I did the job and the Saudis paid me and she had the operation and died anyway. Never even came to after the surgery."

For a few minutes there was no sound except the whine of the truck's engine and the creak of the springs and the rumble of the tires on the dirt road. It was dark now. Some kind of bird flew up from the roadside and flitted through the headlights' beam.

Finally Billy Jumper said, "Been eating you for awhile, has it?"

"Yes."

Although it did seem to have helped matters just telling someone about it. So it was true what they said about confession. It always surprises me when old truisms turn out to be right.

Billy Jumper sighed. "Well," he said, "speaking as a former preacher of the Gospel, I believe God has forgiven you. But I don't have the impression that's what's worrying you."

"Not exactly."

"I wish I was as certain," the old man said, "that you're going to find a way to forgive yourself."

After that neither of us spoke for a long time.

At last he swung the pickup off the road and killed the engine and the lights. "Time to get out and walk," he said softly. "From here on we have to be quiet."

I got down and looked around. The moon was up now, a big half moon hanging a little way above the horizon, and the sky overhead was hung with enormous white stars. It almost seemed light enough to read by. We appeared to be out in the middle of an open plain, covered with some sort of brush and broken by low hills or dunes. There didn't seem to be any houses or manmade structures around.

The old man was motioning to me and I followed him as he set out away from the road down a narrow trail through the brush. I remembered suddenly that this was rattlesnake country, and wished I'd worn boots instead of sneakers. He moved remarkably fast and with no sound at all; it was all I could do to keep from losing him. I wondered just what had really happened in Italy. The world must have lost a great scout when he turned to preaching.

Finally he stopped, holding up a hand in the moonlight, and dropped down beside a bush, motioning me to do the same. He glanced up at the stars for a second and then put his mouth close to my ear and whispered, "Got to wait a little bit."

We sat there, I don't know how long, not moving or speaking. A mosquito landed on my neck and started drilling. Another one started singing around my left ear. Somewhere in the distance an owl hooted.

Suddenly Billy Jumper tapped me on the shoulder and pointed. I looked between the bushes, following his gesture, and for a second I didn't see anything that hadn't been there before. Just a little open area and then more brush. . . .

Then I saw the gray shape moving slowly across the clear area, not much more than a shadow among other shadows. It was about the size of a medium-small dog; in fact as far as I could see at first it *was* a dog. Christ, I thought, he's brought me out here in the middle of the night to look at a stray mutt? But there was something about the way the thing moved, something intangibly but forever and irrevocably wild. Whatever it was, it wasn't a dog.

"Red wolf," Billy Jumper said in my ear.

It was no more than the tiniest, faintest whisper, but it was enough. The wolf stopped, ears pricked up, and then it was moving, flowing soundlessly across the open sandy space, faster than seemed possible for such a skinny, unimpressive-looking creature. It was gone before I'd gotten a really good look at it.

"There, now," Billy Jumper said, "you can tell your grandchildren you saw a red wolf once. Not many people can say that nowadays." He was speaking normally now, rising easily to his feet. "Red wolves are nearly extinct, you know. There's a couple of refuges along the coast, up near Galveston, where they've got a few, but they're almost like animals in a zoo, surrounded by all that industry and development. Not supposed to be any wild ones left this far south. I told the Texas Game and Fish people, and they said I'd been seeing coyotes."

I'd seen a few coyotes myself, out west and down in Mexico. That thing was no coyote.

We started back down the trail toward the road. He said, "I been watching that one and his mate for a couple of years now. I think they got some pups around here somewhere."

As we got back into the truck he said, "Interesting animal, the red wolf. Doesn't run in packs like the big timber wolves up in the North Woods. Pretty much a solitary creature, hunts alone. Nobody knows if this is because his own kind is so rare or just because that's the way he is."

He looked at me before he started the engine. In the dark cab I couldn't see his face.

"I don't know," he said in a neutral voice. "Somehow I just had the idea you might like to see one."

5

• • • • •

BY NOW I WAS GETTING INTO A REGULAR ROU-
tine on the island: run in the morning, swim in the afternoon, listen to the radio or watch old movies on the VCR
in the evening, and sleep like a snake all night. I wasn't
drinking nearly as much now and I'd thrown the pills
away. For company there was Raoul the cat, when he
wasn't off stalking birds among the live-oaks, and now
and then there was a visit from old Billy Jumper, who
also kept me supplied with fresh fish.

It was the most enjoyable time I'd spent in years. Naturally there was no chance it would last.

So I wasn't surprised, about a week after the red wolf
business, when Cameron showed up to tell me somebody
was coming to use the island.

He came roaring and banging across the channel, doing
a clumsy job of piloting one of Billy Jumper's beat-up
flat-bottomed rent-a-yachts. It was a hot afternoon and he
was sweating heavily as he climbed out of the boat and
onto the dock. "Son of a bitch," he said, "I wish I could
get transferred somewhere cooler."

He walked up to the trailer with me and accepted a
cold beer with profuse gratitude. "By God, Dane, you're a
gentleman. . . . Here." He handed me a bundle of newspapers
and magazines. "Thought you might be curious about what's

67

going on in the allegedly real world."

He took a deep pull at his beer and wiped his lips. "Christ, that's good. Not much new, really," he said, gesturing at the bundle. "Some more riots in Rumania. Man, do you believe this shit in Eastern Europe? Even six or seven years ago, if I'd submitted a report that concluded that the whole Communist block from Poland to Bulgaria—Bulgaria, for God's sake!—was going to break apart and start holding free elections, they'd have put me in a padded cell. Even the Russians just said, 'Well, fuck that Communism business, it don't work,' and tossed Marx into the shitcan."

He drank some more beer and laughed. "Only the good old Chinese, God bless 'em, are still holding true to the old evil-ass traditions, and the current administration has decreed that we're not supposed to notice *that*. Wasn't for the crazy Arabs, some of us might be out of work."

He sank into one of the folding chairs in front of the trailer. "Rumania, though, that really warms the cockles, whatever the hell they are—you suppose a cockle is a small cock?—of this old Cold War cowboy's heart. Because the job they did on those bastards, there's no way they didn't nail at least some of the sons of bitches who had so much fun with me back in the good old days. You know they shot Ceausescu?"

"I was in France at the time," I said. "We got full coverage."

"Yeah. Christmas Eve," Cameron said dreamily. "They shot the son of a bitch on Christmas Eve, on national TV. You realize that was the first time they had Christmas in Rumania in years? Ceausescu's boys had outlawed it. So I figure you got all these Rumanian kids, this was the first Christmas they can remember, and when the teacher or the priest asks them if they know what Christmas is all about they'll all say, 'Oh, yes, that's when they shoot the Premier.' "

He drained his beer and smiled with the far-off look of a man contemplating an inner vision too beautiful for words. "Just think," he said. "Little Rudi comes home from school: 'Hey, Mama, I'm in the Christmas play!' 'Oh, are you going to play Premier Ceausescu?' 'No, but I'm one of the firing squad.' I bet they put out little firing-squad scenes with toy soldiers under the tree instead of the manger scene."

I hated to cut in while he was on a roll—from what I'd heard, he'd more than earned the right to this particular one—but I said, "Excuse me, but was there something you came out here for? Besides discussing current events?"

"Oh, sure. Sorry." He tossed the empty onto the sand, barely missing Raoul, who was sleeping in the shade of the trailer. "Hey, where'd the cat come from?"

"I would guess," I said, "the same place they all come from."

"You're probably right. I tend to forget about pussy, at my age. Which," he said, "sort of brings us, indirectly, to what I came to tell you. You're about to have company on the island."

He took off his hat and rubbed his head. "Actually I'm pretty sure you're going to have to check out for awhile. I don't think the people who're coming are going to want to share the place."

"Some kind of top-secret Company business?"

"Not exactly. Although it's sure as hell secret, but not in the way you're used to." He looked up at the house on its tall pilings. "That's right, you're gonna have to do some work in the next few days—get that plywood off the windows, make sure everything's working. Well, it's about time you earned your keep."

He folded his hands over his stomach and gazed blandly at me. "I don't know if you ever heard of United States Representative Jerry Raintree."

"Heard of him," I said, "that's about all. I couldn't even tell you what party he belongs to."

"Immaterial. The important thing, from your point of view, is that Congressman Raintree is one of the friendlies. Sits on the House Intelligence Committee and has several pretty tight buddies in fairly high Company echelons. One of the few moderates on the Hill who doesn't make a hobby out of beating up the CIA."

I said, "I think I'm starting to see this coming."

"You probably are, son. Raintree's friends in the Company were only too happy to do him a little favor. Seems he has need of a quiet, out-of-the-way place to spend a few off-the-record days."

"Somewhere safe from casual observation? And maybe safe from the press?"

Cameron smiled in a fatherly way. "By George, I think you got it."

"Christ." I sat down in the other chair. "What is it in Raintree's case? Booze, boys, or bimbos?"

"As far as I know, only Number Three. Never heard he had any sort of bottle problem, and he definitely likes girls. Unfortunately," Cameron said, "he's got a lady already. And a very damn well-known one. Mrs. Raintree is extremely popular in her home state *and* nationally, appears on TV, writes articles in the women's magazines—or signs her name to them, anyway—even has a book coming out next year. Loved by feminists and traditionalists alike. Any public revelation that Jerry Raintree is doing her wrong—"

"Ah."

"Yes. So Jerry can't just trot off to the nearest No-Tell Motel with his hot patootie of the month. He's already had some close calls. This is the ideal setup for him. Naturally he's been told that you're absolutely reliable in terms of discretion."

I said, "You think his wife doesn't already know?"

"If she's as smart as everybody says, she probably does. But knowing about it is one thing. Having it blow up in the national press, so you can't pretend any longer, is something else. Anyway," Cameron said, "ours not to reason why or even how. Yours to get the house livable by next weekend. Mine to go back to Houston and hope nothing goes wrong. Don't let anything go wrong, Dane." He hoisted himself reluctantly out of the chair. "I only got a couple of years to go to retirement."

Down at the dock he paused for a last look around. "Sorry to do this to you, Dane," he said. "Had yourself a pretty soft deal here for awhile, didn't you? Of course a lot of men would have gone nuts out here alone, but from all I've heard I don't think that bothers you."

I said, "Nobody knows whether the red wolf is solitary because there are so few of his kind, or just because that's the way he is."

"What?" Cameron looked baffled.

"Nothing. I was . . . thinking of something."

He shook his head. "Maybe you *have* been out here too long."

Still shaking his head, he got back into the boat and untied the line from the dock. A few minutes later he was a black dot on the sun-bright surface of the bay, growing rapidly smaller as he headed back toward Bayport. I watched until I couldn't see him any more and then I went back up to the house and got to work.

I stayed busy for the next few days. The work wasn't all that bad, but in the heat it wasn't a lot of laughs either.

It didn't help, I suppose, that I was doing it all for no better reason than to allow some politician to spend a little interlude getting into what used to be called strange stuff. I felt like the manager of a cheap motel—and, as I struggled with the heavy sheets of plywood in the hot sun, I had a little more sympathy for Norman Bates. Maybe people had judged the guy too harshly.

I wrestled the plywood panels off the windows—the nails that held them were balky with rust—and stacked them underneath the house. I didn't want to think how short a time it would probably be before I had to put them back up. I was definitely going to have to get back to my usual line of work; I wasn't cut out for a custodial career.

Billy Jumper showed up while I was stacking the plywood. "Moving into the house?" he inquired.

I shook my head and wiped away sweat. "Somebody's going to be using it for awhile. Not me."

"Huh. They flying in?"

"I don't know. Why?"

"Oh, something I saw this morning. Big seaplane moored in a lagoon down south of here—not a floatplane but the kind that sits down on the water, you know?"

"Flying boat?"

"That's it. Not a *great* big one, you understand, not as big as those PBY's we used to see during the war, but it had two motors and I guess it would hold a good many men. There were these two Zodiac boats tied up alongside, you know what a Zodiac is?"

"High-performance inflatable, sure." They're extremely popular in the international skulduggery business, for obvious reasons. Whether you're a dope smuggler or a mercenary or just the hard-working local representative of somebody's secret agency, the Zodiac is very much the watercraft of choice. I thought once about trying to get the dealership for the eastern Mediterranean, but some people had beaten me to it.

"Nice-looking plane," Billy Jumper said, "painted light blue, no markings that I could see. Some men fooling around in the boats, I didn't get close enough to see them clear. I thought maybe it was some dope runners, better stay away."

"Probably right." I didn't know much about local affairs but it figured that this would be a prime stretch of coast for dopers, smugglers of illegal aliens, and other activities best left unprobed. "Did they see you?"

"No. I got out of there."

If Billy Jumper said they didn't see him, they didn't. I wasn't surprised.

"But anyway," he said, "I thought it might have something to do with whoever you're expecting."

"No. This guy isn't coming until the weekend. Anyway, there's no reason he'd be fooling around in some remote lagoon."

Billy Jumper looked at the stack of plywood. "I could probably find you a couple of local boys," he said, "do the work for you for beer money. Lot of unemployment around here."

It was a temptation, but Cameron would have a fit if I brought outsiders onto the island. I said, "Thanks. I can handle it."

As he motored away, I wondered briefly if I ought to report what he'd seen. The seaplane with no markings sounded suspicious as hell; it was unlikely to be Company business but no doubt Cameron could relay the information to whatever Federal agency was likely to be interested. But the hell with it, I decided. I wasn't a cop, and right now my employment by the Company was strictly jackass labor. Let the DEA and the Coast Guard worry about it.

• • •

I got the house cleaned up and the plumbing working; there was nothing much wrong beyond a leaky toilet tank that required a bit of adjustment, and a bit of sand here and there on the floors. I checked the big buried storage tanks that held fresh water and the supply of diesel fuel for the generator; both were nearly full, which was a relief, since I had no idea what arrangements the Company had for getting them refilled. There was no gas supply to worry about, the kitchens in both the house and the trailer being all-electric—although somehow I had a feeling that next week's occupants weren't going to be doing a lot of cooking.

I was replacing the cover on the fuel tank when I heard a boat coming up the channel, headed toward the island. I went down to the dock and watched as a big inflatable came bouncing across the waves, planing along in front of some sort of fairly serious motor. A Zodiac; there's no mistaking them once you've seen one. I remembered Billy Jumper's story about the strange seaplane, and wished I'd brought a gun with me.

It was too late now, though. The Zodiac was already coming in, engine throttled back to dog-paddle speed, and a big dark-skinned man was standing in the bow waving at me.

He shouted, "Hello! Hello! Please, one minute!"

He wore only blue nylon shorts; he had the massive chest and shoulders of a wrestler or a weight lifter, and his skin was darker than Billy Jumper's. He had curly black hair and a mustache and as hairy a chest as I'd ever seen. Right now he was displaying a lot of very white teeth.

As the Zodiac nosed up to the dock he said, "Please, you are living on this island? Yes?"

There were three other men in the boat with him. They were all of generally similar appearance; one had a beard but otherwise they looked damn near interchangeable. I hadn't seen so many big muscles and great tans since the last time I was on the Riviera. They could have posed for a health-club advertisement.

I said, "I live here now."

"Ah. Very good." His accent was strong but not thick. At first I'd figured my visitors for Mexicans, or other Hispanic types, but this wasn't anything like a Mexican accent. It did sound very familiar, though.

The one in the bow said, "May we come ashore, please?"

I said, "What was it you wanted?"

"Yes. Well." He moved his lips slightly as if getting the words right. "We, ah—represent? Represent, yes. We represent a certain person who is interested in properties along this coast. He is wishing to buy for development." Actually he said "dewelopment." I was fairly sure I had the accent pegged now. "He is especially interested in islands such as this."

The one with the beard said, "We want to look."

"Yes. We would like to have a look at this island, if you will permit?" He reached out toward the dock.

I said, "Sorry. I just take care of the place. I don't have any authority to let anyone look around."

"But surely—"

"No. Sorry. It wouldn't do you any good anyway," I said. "The island is the property of the United States government."

The one with the beard said impatiently, "In the name of God, Ali, get on with it."

It took me by surprise, though by now I ought to have been ready for it. But who expects to hear a man speaking Arabic on the Texas coast?

Without turning to look at him Ali said in the same language, "Be quiet, Gamal. Let me do this. The man is no more than a hired caretaker."

To me, in English, he said, "Even so, we are still interested. Sometimes government properties can be bought, you know? Our employer, he has many good friends in Washington."

I shook my head. "Sorry."

I was starting to feel like an idiot, standing there saying the same thing over and over. It came to me that this was probably one reason cops and security guards got so cranky.

Ali's smile grew downright blinding. "But sir, who is to know if you merely let us walk about the island a little? You may watch us, we will only take a few photographs. And," he added with a sly expression, "we would make it profitable for you, you understand?" He made a thumb-across-fingers gesture. "A little something for your trouble?"

I shook my head again. If this went on much longer I was going to have a sore neck. And if these characters didn't back off pretty soon I was going to go get the shotgun and the hell with public relations. No Texas jury would convict a man for shooting an Arab anyway, after the games they'd been playing with oil prices.

Gamal started to speak but Ali cut him off. "It does not matter," he said in Arabic. "It is not worth making trouble. We have already seen enough here."

Gamal looked pissed off, but he shrugged and bent over the motor. Ali said, "Well, good day, sir." In Arabic, still smiling, he added several remarks concerning my appearance, habits, and probable relationship with my mother.

I stopped myself from responding in kind—it would have been fun to see his face, but the guns were in the trailer and I didn't need to be mixing it up barehanded with this collection of Mediterranean Muscle Beach types. Instead I stood there on the dock looking dumb while they backed the Zodiac away from the dock and turned it sharply toward open water.

They swung through a big circle, picking up speed, and came blasting back past me, going full out by now. One of the men was pointing a black object at me and I started to dive off the dock, but then I saw it was only a camera. A few minutes later there remained no sign of them except the rush of their wake against the beach and, far off down the channel to the south, the roar of their motor.

Cameron said, "I wouldn't worry about it."

It had taken me over an hour to reach him on the balky radiotelephone in the house.

"I know what's bothering you," he said, "but let's not let our prejudices make us panic here. Hard as it is for a lot of us to keep in mind, there *are* plenty of Arab-type people with perfectly legitimate business in this country. I mean, they aren't *all* in El Fatah or Black September or Hezbollah."

I said, "Well, hell, Cameron, I just figured you'd want to be told. Under the circumstances."

I hadn't actually mentioned the Congressman's coming visit. I didn't know who might be listening in. Few communications are as leaky as radiotelephone. We were both doing a certain amount of talking around corners.

"I do want to know," Cameron's voice said in my ear. "I'm glad you called. All I'm saying, I don't think this is anything to get worried about. There actually are some Arabs trying to buy up coastal real estate up around Galveston, though I don't know how much luck they've had. Even if these jokers are into something shady, though," he went on, "it's probably dope or something. Hell, they might even be old buddies of the guy who used to own the island. Plenty of possible reasons somebody might have a use for a place like that."

I said, "So you don't think this is . . . going to change anything?" Dammit, why couldn't they have put a scrambler on this thing?

He laughed. "Afraid not, Dane. You don't get off that easy."

I wondered if he thought I was exaggerating in the hope of getting Raintree to cancel. I might have, if I'd thought of it. Should have told them they were brandishing AK's and the Ayatollah's picture. Or Washington *Post* credentials; that would have done it for sure. . . .

"I'll look into it," he added. "Might get some people to look for that blue seaplane, at least, though I wouldn't expect much—they got everybody stretched out thin with this war-on-drugs business. And I'll see if anybody knows anything about any ragheads in the area. Shit, maybe we *will* sell them the place, they make a good enough offer. After all, we got it free."

After he had hung up I went back to the trailer and sat for awhile in the shade drinking beer and scratching Raoul's ears and thinking. Finally I decided Cameron was right; I was getting jumpy over nothing. I'd been in the Middle East too long, been shot at too many times by people who spoke Arabic. Evidently my nerves still hadn't settled down. I reminded myself that I'd had some damn good friends who spoke that language.

I said, "Raoul, I'm turning into an old lady seeing rapists behind every tree."

Raoul closed his eyes and began one of his seismic purrs. Get a couple more like him going at the same time and they'd shake the leaves off the live-oaks.

I watched him for a minute and decided he had the right attitude. I said, "I'm with you, Raoul. The hell with them." And got up and went inside to fix the fish Billy Jumper had brought over earlier in the day, and give my paranoia a much-needed rest.

All the same, I kept a gun handy from then on.

Friday afternoon the Congressman arrived. As promised, he brought someone along.

6

•••••

SHE WASN'T WHAT I'D EXPECTED. I'M NOT SURE just what I *had* been expecting, but she wasn't it.

She got out of the little gray car and came striding across the parking area in back of Billy Jumper's boat shed, her heels making sharp crunching sounds in the gravel. She said, "Dane? Are you Dane?"

As she came toward me I saw that she was small, not over five feet tall. Make that short; some parts of her weren't small at all. There was a lot of chest under her white blouse and all of it was in vigorous motion.

Behind me, sitting on an oil drum, Billy Jumper said softly, "My, my. Looks like she's got a couple of pet raccoon cubs in there. Playful little cusses, too."

Actually my first reaction was to wonder what all the fuss was about. Knockers aside—and they weren't all *that* remarkable—she had a decent figure but nothing world-class; and as she came closer I saw that she had a snub nose and a wide mouth. Her white-blonde hair was cut short, not very well—although for all I knew the ragged look was in this year—and she had on too much eye shadow. All in all, I couldn't see anything to make a man risk his career.

She stopped in front of me and I said, "I'm Dane." She was looking around nervously and I added, "It's all clear. He can get out of the car."

81

She bobbed her head and started back toward the car. Headed away from me in those tight jeans, she presented an interesting view, and I revised my initial opinion somewhat. Billy Jumper murmured, "By God, she's got a regular *zoo* in her clothes."

I said, "Quiet, you dirty old man. You're not even supposed to be seeing these people."

"What people?" he said innocently. "I don't see a soul."

The woman was bending over the car—that was worth watching—and speaking to someone inside. A moment later the left-hand door opened and Jerry Raintree climbed out.

He didn't fit my expectations either, though I'd seen his picture in the magazines Cameron had brought. He certainly wasn't dressed very Congressionally. He had on faded jeans and running shoes and a blue tennis shirt, with a mesh-backed cap pulled down low over his eyes. The cap bore a picture of a leaping bass and the logo of a fishing-tackle manufacturer. A pair of mirror shades completed the job of hiding the upper half of his face.

He looked like a minor-league baseball coach, or a Southern city cop about to start his vacation—which, no doubt, was the idea; even in this place, there was always the risk of recognition. He appeared fit and muscular, and younger than his forty-some years; he moved quickly and athletically across the parking lot toward me, smiling and extending his hand. When he did that he suddenly looked like a politician again, but I took his hand anyway.

He said, "You're Dane? Sorry I'm a bit late, but we had some delays coming down. Damn airlines haven't been able to get things right since deregulation." He looked around at what there was of Bayport. "Hell of a place to have to wait."

Then he looked past me and said, "Ah, excuse me—"

I said, "It's all right. This is Billy Jumper. He owns this

boat dock and he's completely trustworthy. He's okay," I
added sharply, as Raintree hesitated. I could see his problem, but all this paranoia was getting to me. "You can leave
your car here, he'll keep an eye on it."

I wondered whose car it really was. Raintree might simply have rented it at the airport—Houston, I assumed—
but I suspected this was yet another little favor from his
Company pals. If they could lend him an entire island, a
set of wheels should be no big deal.

He said, "Well, all right." He took the blonde's arm.
"This is Brenda."

I doubted it very seriously, but I looked at her and said,
"Pleased to meet you," or something equally original. He
didn't supply a last name. She didn't speak at all.

"Okay," I said, "we better get your stuff out of the
car."

It took a second before he realized that "we" included
him—I might be a caretaker for the moment, but I was
damned if I'd play porter too—and then he nodded and
we headed for the car. Billy Jumper came along, unasked,
and the three of us got the suitcases out of the trunk and
down to the dock.

I climbed down into the skiff and stowed the bags as
they passed them down to me. There wasn't nearly as much
junk as I'd expected; they were traveling light for a week's
trip. But then Raintree had been doing a sneak and a lot
of luggage might have raised questions, and Brenda wasn't
going to have a lot of occasion to dress up around here—not
that that would have stopped a lot of women I'd known.

I wondered how they'd handled the logistics of their
little adventure. Probably took separate flights to Houston,
picked up the car and drove down to Bayport. I wasn't
really knowledgeable about such matters. I won't say I
never got over the line during the three years I was married,

but it was strictly spur-of-the-moment action. I never had been involved in one of these elaborate extended affairs. It always seemed to me that married life was complicated enough as it was. But then my face wasn't on the cover of *People* magazine.

That had been a neat little touch, though, letting her get out of the car and check out the situation before he showed his own famous face. Nice to see that chivalry was still alive among our elected representatives.

Brenda climbed awkwardly down the ladder; she was wearing white sandals with big heels, about as impractical a choice as you could devise for getting in and out of a small boat. I took her hand to steady her as she sat down. Her grip was tight and nervous; obviously she wasn't at all comfortable about boat rides. Raintree came down, moving lightly and easily, and untied our line and coiled it neatly— I remembered reading that he'd been in the Navy—before sitting down beside her. I gunned the motor and we headed out across the bay, with Billy Jumper trailing along behind us in his old flat-bottomed boat, getting bounced around by our wake but not seeming to mind.

Raintree jerked a thumb back at Billy and tilted his head. I said, "He'll be bringing me back to the mainland once we've got you moved in. That is if that's what you want me to do."

He took off his silly damn gimme cap and grinned at me. He looked more like his photos now: the curly dark hair, the gleaming smile, the features that all the journalists liked to describe as "craggy." A pretty boy, but no more so, as far as I could see, than most of the other pols of his age group. Poor George Washington, with his big nose and his lumpy dentures, wouldn't have a chance nowadays.

Raintree said, "Well, to be candid, that *was* pretty much the arrangement we had in mind. If it's all right with you?

You've got somewhere you can go?"

"There's a motel in Bayport. You probably saw it."

"Yes. Well, I'll certainly be glad to cover your bill. Sorry for the inconvenience."

Brenda was pointing with one hand and shading her eyes with the other. "Is that the island? It looks so tiny."

Raintree said, "Big enough for us," and gave her a suggestive look. He added something in her ear and she hit him lightly on the knee.

I decided I didn't mind moving into the motel after all. There was no way I could spend a week on that island with these two oversexed characters; it would be embarrassing. It was bad enough watching them right now. I felt like the chauffeur in one of those romantic comedies, trying not to watch in the rear-view mirror while his boss pulls the secretary's panties down.

I opened the throttle wider, until the engine noise drowned out further speech. Any minute, I thought, they were going to start giggling, and I didn't want to hear it.

When we had everything unloaded and carried up to the house, Brenda announced that she was going to take a shower. I shut off the mental images as best I could and said to Raintree, "I better show you around."

We went down the steps and out to the blockhouse. I showed him how to keep the generator running and he seemed to pick it up quickly; I'd been afraid he'd be one of those hopelessly un-mechanical nitwits who'd keep me running out here every day to screw in light bulbs or change the toilet roll. "It's pretty reliable," I said. "You shouldn't have to fool with it."

He looked around. "Well-built structures," he said. "This can't possibly be government-contract work."

"It was built by a drug dealer originally."

"Oh?" He made a face. "And of course it was confiscated well before the owner actually went to trial, along with everything else he owned. That's how it works nowadays, never mind the old-fashioned notion that a man is innocent until proven guilty. Even if you're acquitted, it's nearly impossible to make them give your property back. My God," he said, "I don't minimize the drug problem, but it's become the pretext for the most outrageous abuses, the most hypocritical grandstanding . . . but it's political suicide to say so right now. Well." He sighed. "I'm supposedly on a vacation and here I am making speeches."

I said, "There's not much food in the house except canned stuff. If you'd like to make out a list of what you want, I'll give it to Billy."

"Billy?"

"The old Indian. The thing is," I said, "the store in Bayport doesn't have much of a selection, but there's a supermarket in Soto, and Billy's got a pickup truck." And could use a little of your money.

"Hm. Good. Certainly. I'll go up to the house," Raintree said, "and see what Brenda wants. Back in a couple of minutes."

While he was gone I went to the trailer and stuffed some clothes and personal junk into a duffel bag. I picked up the .44 from the bedside table and bounced it in my hand, considering. I couldn't think of any reason I was likely to need it in Bayport, but anything was possible. I shoved it into the bag too.

Raintree appeared, holding a folded sheet of paper. "The list," he said. "Tell him I'll reimburse him when he brings it, and I'll make it worth his time."

I said, "Hang on. I just thought of something."

I went back into the trailer and got the shotgun and the shells. "Here," I said. "This goes in that cabinet up at the

house. I had some trouble with some local punks. Don't
think they'll be back but you never know."

He held the shotgun and studied it, grinning. "I really
can't see myself using this," he said. "I'm supposed to
communicate with people, you know, not shoot them. Have
meaningful dialogues with them," he added drily. "But if it
makes you feel better I'll take this thing."

He tucked the gun under his left arm and stuck out
his hand. "Well, thanks for everything, Dane. See you in
a week."

I went down to the dock, lugging my duffel bag, and
climbed into Billy Jumper's boat, and we went buzzing
off toward the mainland. I looked back at the house but
I couldn't see either of them.

Billy Jumper began singing in a high voice:

> *"Heliluyen yuhikuthles*
> *Heli heliluyen—"*

I said, "Here. They want you to go up to Soto and buy
them some groceries. As your manager I advise you to soak
them."

The old man took the list and stuffed it into his pocket,
giving me a toothless smile. He continued singing:

> *"Mekosapulket mimon opothles*
> *Heli heliluyen—"*

I wondered what the words meant. Probably Seminole
for "It's going to be a long week, white man."

The motel owner was only too happy to get an all-week
customer; he gave me my pick of the shabby little rooms.
The place was all but empty. The few guests seemed to

spend most of their time fishing on the bay.

I hung up my clothes and laid the .44 on the dresser. The powder and caps were still on the island; I should have told Raintree not to smoke around the storeroom. If he smoked; I couldn't remember seeing him light up. But then I remembered the shape of Brenda's rolling buttocks under that taut-stretched denim and decided Raintree wasn't likely to do a lot of wandering around. He might never even get out of the house.

The rattling old air conditioner finally began to cool the room down to something bearable. I flipped on the television to kill a little time before dinner. That turned out to be a waste of time; the local cable carried nothing but the regular network shows, a pop-music channel for sociopathic teenagers, and reruns of such stunners as *The Big Valley* and *Petticoat Junction*. There was also a sports channel, but my set wouldn't pick it up properly; I got the announcer's voice but not the picture, which was the exact opposite of what I wanted.

I sat there on the bed awhile flipping the dial, fascinated in spite of myself. It was the first time I'd seen any of the talk shows; they'd been in their infancy the last time I'd been in the States. There was a white-haired geek who rushed hysterically about the studio, whining and waving his arms and interrupting everyone who tried to speak; there was a really obnoxious Hispanic type who went in heavily for striking poses and staring melodramatically into the camera; and there was a tiny birdlike woman with huge glasses who looked exactly like my fourth-grade teacher and didn't seem to have a clue what anyone was talking about. There was also a heavyish, pleasant-faced black woman who gave the impression of being acutely embarrassed by what she was doing for a living.

All the shows featured a bunch of pompous waterheads

sitting on a stage, spouting incomprehensible bullshit, and an audience bussed in from the nearest home for the brain-damaged. I flipped off the TV and lay back on the bed, remembering a bumper sticker I'd seen in Washington: BEAM ME UP, SCOTTY, THERE'S NO INTELLIGENT LIFE HERE.

After awhile I dozed off, made lethargic by the heat and the recent overdose of dumb. And dreamed a strange, terrible dream: a nude mud-wrestling tag-team match, Phil Donahue and Sally Jessy Raphael against Geraldo Rivera and Oprah Winfrey. I was trying to get a bet down on Geraldo and Oprah, who clearly had the weight advantage, when Jerry Raintree and Brenda showed up at ringside, also naked, and offered to take on the winners. . . .

I woke up, sweating and foul-breathed, and went into the tiny bathroom and stuck my head under the shower a few minutes. Then I left the motel and walked down the road to Billy Jumper's place.

I found him in the weed-grown lot next to his boat shed, shooting arrows at a cornstalk target. "*Umhisse*," he said genially when he saw me, and held out the bow. "Like to try?"

I said, "Hell, I wouldn't even know how to hold this thing."

But I took it anyway, and looked it over carefully; weapons of any sort always interest me. It wasn't one of the modern bows with the pulleys and the cat's-cradle strings, or even a fiberglass model; this was a real old-fashioned Indian bow, obviously hand-made, of some hard yellowish-brown wood. "You made this?" I asked.

"Uh huh. That's what we call bodark wood. From the French *bois d'arc*, meaning bow wood, oddly enough. Or so a professor told me once back in seminary."

I pulled casually at the string, and then less casually. Not much happened; the string had decided to remain unpulled.

Christ, the old man must have muscles like a snake to pull this thing. I handed it back and he took an arrow from a quiver on his belt. Even I could see that the arrow was also handmade, fletched with what looked like turkey feathers. "Watch me miss it," he said.

The bow came up and he hauled back the string easily as a woman pulling down a windowshade. He didn't appear to sight down the arrow like a modern archer; he just steadied down and let go. The arrow whipped across the lot and hit the bundle of cornstalks dead center with an audible *whuck*.

I said, "Now I understand why the Seminole War lasted so long. I'd hate to have you after me with that thing."

He laughed. "Well, like I told you, it's just a hobby. Do a little hunting now and then, little bowfishing if the warden isn't around. Mostly just kill cornstalks. Takes me back, you know," he said, unstringing the bow. "When I was a boy in Oklahoma we still hunted small game with these things. Bullets cost way too much to waste on squirrels and birds and suchlike."

I said, "When are you going for the Horny Couple's groceries?"

He gave me an odd look. "Already been and gone. Got back from the island nearly an hour ago."

I looked at the sun. For God's sake, it was almost to the horizon. I'd slept longer than I'd realized.

"You ought to have come," Billy Jumper went on. "Boy, that woman looked nice in that little black bathing suit. What there was of it. Just three little patches of cloth and some string. Man, there wasn't anything like that around when *I* was that age, I can guarantee you."

"Maybe you don't remember."

"Nope. If there had of been, I'd never got to be *this* age."

I said, "Want to go to Soto and see if we can find a place open, get some burgers or fried chicken or something? I'm buying."

"Seems like everybody's throwing their money my way today," he said. "I got a better idea. Let me go get my arrows and we'll go to my place, and I'll fix us up a mess of fish and potatoes."

I walked with him to the target. All his arrows were bunched into an area I could have covered with my hand without opening my fingers.

He stopped, hand on an arrow shaft, and turned his head this way and that, sniffing the air. "Storm on the way," he said. "Not a big one, not a hurricane, but there's gonna be a storm in a few days. Bet on it."

The sky was clear and none of the radio or TV forecasts had said anything about a storm, but I said, "Should I warn those two out on the island?"

He spat into the grass. "Hell, son," he said, "even if the roof blows off, they'll never notice it. . . ."

But there was one thing that could still get Jerry Raintree's attention, something that no woman would ever replace in his list of priorities.

There were no telephones in the motel rooms. I was awakened Monday morning by the manager banging on my door.

"You got a phone call," he said when I finally got up and peered out at him. "In the office."

The voice on the phone was female, the connection shitty; it took me a minute to realize that it was Brenda. "Dane," she said, "listen, he's got to go somewhere. It's an emergency."

I wondered why Raintree couldn't have talked to me himself. Maybe he was used to having a woman place his calls for him, though if Brenda was a secretary I was Idi Amin. More likely he was just afraid someone would recognize his voice. Well, radiotelephones *are* a pretty public means of communication, especially in a coastal area where you've got a lot of marine sets—some salt-water types make a regular hobby of eavesdropping on RT conversations—but hell, he wasn't that famous, not in Texas anyway. And besides, on that set you'd have had a hard time recognizing Elvis Presley.

I said, "Am I supposed to come get him or something?"

"No, he's bringing the skiff over. He wants you to meet him," Brenda said, "down at the boat dock. Make sure, you know, there's nobody around when he gets there."

"When's he coming?" I asked a little irritably.

She said, "He's about to leave right now."

I hung up the phone and handed it back to the manager and went outside. The sky was overcast. Heavy banks of cloud were moving in from out at sea, but the brightish patch in the eastern sky told me the sun had been up for quite awhile. Should have been out of bed long before this, but I'd sat up late watching an old Lee Marvin movie on the late show: *The Professionals*, still one of the best flicks ever made. . . .

What the hell kind of wild hair did Raintree have up his ass now? Maybe he'd run out of rubbers. Or "condoms" as everybody was calling them on the TV talk shows. Actually the preferred prissy term seemed to be "safe sex," which struck me as containing an internal contradiction, like "military intelligence."

By the time I got down to the boat dock I could see him coming in, steering the skiff a little awkwardly but well enough for the conditions. He tossed the line up to me and I secured it as he climbed the ladder, looking nervously around. He had on his silly-bastard cap again, and the mirror shades. He also had a little nylon carry-on airline bag slung over his shoulder by a web strap.

He said, "Dane, I got a message early this morning from my staff back in Washington. Or rather Cameron got it and relayed it to me. I've got to fly back for a couple of days."

"Congressional business?"

He nodded. "There's an important bill coming up for a vote and I've got to be there. It wasn't supposed to come up on the floor for another week, but the people pushing it did some cute things that—well, never mind. Believe me, if I told you the details, you'd want it stopped as badly as I do."

I had my doubts about that, but I nodded to be polite. I said, "Brenda's not coming?"

"Oh, no. I'll be back Wednesday or Thursday. She might as well stay here and enjoy herself." And, of course, if she went with him it increased the risk of their getting spotted together.

He looked at the sky, frowning. "Storm coming, isn't there?"

"So Billy Jumper says, and he's usually right."

"Hm. But no hurricane warnings out, according to the radio. Still. . . ." He gave me an embarrassed look. "Would it be too much of an imposition if I asked you to move back out to the island until I get back? I'd feel a lot better knowing you were there. If a really bad storm or other emergency came up, she could never get the skiff over here on her own."

I said, "Sure. No problem." Anything to get away from the Bayport Motel and the idiot tube. "I'll go get my stuff," I added.

"Well, come on, no use walking half a mile, I'll drop you off." He led the way to the little gray car, which was now even grayer with an accumulation of coastal-plain dust. "You probably think it's stupid," he said as we got in, "rushing off like this, interrupting my leisure time to go hassle over legislation. Tell you the truth, sometimes I think it's stupid myself."

He started the engine and leaned back, hands on the wheel, a tired look on his face. "It's such a lot of bullshit, Dane," he said suddenly. "We run around the Hill playing at running the country, but we don't run a damned thing but our mouths. The President doesn't run the country either, though that's the general perception."

He looked at me, his mouth not quite smiling. "There's a widespread belief among the liberals that you people in the CIA and other secret agencies are actually running things, but you know what nonsense that is. The sinister CIA is just as muddled as everyone else."

I didn't bother to correct his mistake; let him think I was CIA if it suited him. He was right about the rest of it, though. The Company, like most other Federal agencies, had long since vanished up its own ass in a cloud of bureaucratic confusion. I ought to know.

"As for the popular legend that big business and the very rich run the country, or the world," he added, putting the car into reverse, "events on Wall Street and elsewhere ought to have dispelled *that* notion for good. My God, the private sector is even more fucked up than the government."

I said, "So who *is* running things?"

"Nobody." His shoulders slumped. "People don't run things any more, Dane, things run us. It's all out of control. Maybe the science fiction stories are right; maybe the computers are secretly ruling the world. God knows I'd like to believe *something* knows what's going on." His mouth made a smile that never got to the rest of his face. "You know why they call Congress a legislative body? Because it acts like something with no head."

He was certainly in a state today. I said, "So why go running off to Washington if it doesn't make any difference?"

"Because you have to do something," he said, pulling out onto the dusty road. "You have to act as if you're making some sort of difference, even if you know deep down that it's a shabby farce. Surely in your line of work you've had similar feelings."

"I suppose." I didn't want to discuss my own occupational hangups. I wasn't really interested in his, for that matter, but he seemed to need to talk to somebody. I said, "I've never been involved in trying to solve any of the world's great problems."

After a moment I added, "Unless it would be over-population."

He gave me a quick and very strange look, but he didn't say any more. A few minutes later I was standing in front of the motel, watching his car disappear up the road toward Houston.

7

• • • • •

BY THE TIME I GOT BACK OUT TO THE ISLAND
the clouds were dense and dark, hanging low in the sky,
marching steadily in from seaward with the inexorable
purposefulness of infantry advancing over open ground.
The wind was starting to pick up, too, though not yet
enough to make problems. The waves were higher in the
channel and spray broke over the skiff's bow and wet my
face as I headed in. I put in a little extra work with the
mooring lines before I went ashore. If this got really serious
nothing I could do would keep the storm from taking the
skiff; but if it got that bad, an open skiff wouldn't be any
use to me anyway.

Raoul ran up as I unlocked the trailer and followed
me inside with a ragged yowl. I said, "Getting along all
right with our guests?" and he switched his tail and said
something bitter about not getting fed. But when I went
back outside there were a couple of freshly-emptied tuna
fish cans on the sand. I scratched his ears and said, "You
lying old bastard. You're turning into a real Company
cat."

Brenda's voice said, "Dane? Is that you?"

I looked around and then up. She was hanging over the
railing of the sun deck, looking down at me. All she had
on was a black string bikini and a pair of shades.

"Hi," she said. "I was afraid I was going to be marooned on this damn desert island alone."

She turned and disappeared from my view. A moment later she came bouncing down the steps. "Did Jerry send you out to keep an eye on me?"

She walked past me, looking up at the sky, her movements restless. She said, "I guess the sun won't be coming out at all today, will it?"

"No. There's going to be a storm, probably this evening late."

"Jerry said something about that. I wasn't listening. . . . Oh well, I don't tan worth a damn anyway." She ran her hand over her face and then along her thigh. "Son of a bitch, but it's hot. Steamy. Like those clouds are just holding the heat in on top of us."

If she'd been working on a tan she hadn't made much progress that I could see. And I could see pretty much all there was; the little bit she had on wasn't covering enough to make any difference. The "suit" consisted of two tiny triangles of black fabric, that covered her nipples and not much else, and a larger one hauled up between her legs, plus enough string to hold everything more or less in place. From behind, you couldn't see anything but string; the bottom part vanished between her buttocks, so that if she wasn't quite naked she was definitely bare-assed. Her skin was white; she couldn't have been out in the sun much in that rig or she'd have been burned red as a lobster by now. As it was, a few pinkish areas on her back and bottom indicated she'd come pretty close.

She turned and saw me looking at her. She gave me a slow smile and pushed her shades up onto her forehead. Her eyes said, "What are *you* looking at?"

Actually, while her present ensemble might have been enough to get Billy Jumper's geriatric juices pumping, it wasn't all that daring by modern standards; and I was used to European beaches, where she would have been considered seriously overdressed. Along much of the Riviera topless is practically standard and bottomless isn't unknown— but she was right, all the same; I *was* enjoying the view. She was one of the few women I'd seen who actually looked better with her clothes off.

Raoul appeared, rubbing against her ankles. "Your cat?" she said.

"I don't think he's anybody's cat," I said. "I think he's a free lance."

"Should have told Jerry," she said. "He's got some kind of allergy, breaks out if he gets around animals. Goes through all kind of hell when he's campaigning, has to pose for the cameras petting some kid's puppy or looking over some farmer's cows. Only survives with a lot of injections. He just about shit when he saw this cat here."

She leaned against the trailer, facing me. A droplet of sweat ran down across her belly, leaving a shiny track. "Wish I could go for a swim, but the water's too rough, I guess. . . ."

I opened the trailer door. "Like a beer?" I said over my shoulder.

"Sure. If it's cold. I could stand a change from Scotch, or those wines with the screwy names."

I brought out a couple of cans of Lone Star and handed her one. "Thanks . . . never saw this brand in cans before," she said, checking the label.

"Down here it hardly ever comes any other way. Where did you ever drink Lone Star? You don't sound like a Texan."

"Christ, you don't get around much, do you? How long have you been on this island?" She took a swallow of beer and wiped her lips. "Man, this is a big status drink in certain circles around Washington and New York and Chi. Almost as big a deal as Mexican beer with some of these upwardly-mobile assholes, the kind of macho-man suits who keep a Harley in the garage next to the Mercedes and say things like 'go for it.' But it's got to be in long-necked bottles."

Her mouth twisted. "Even Jerry's got a touch of that bug," she said. "Not enough to play those phony cowboy games, but now and then it shows through."

She looked at me with large long-lashed eyes. They were an interesting deep blue, almost violet. "You don't know," she said, "but it's been a big rush for him, having a real CIA man on call. Makes him feel like James Bond or somebody."

I nodded and drank my beer. Maybe I should tell her that I wasn't a CIA agent, but it didn't seem to matter. I knew what she was talking about, though. It wasn't all that uncommon. The Company had developed a regular little production number out of it: pick out the politician with the swing vote on the committee, bring him over to Langley for a "briefing" featuring lots of impressive-looking but unimportant classified information, maybe stage a demonstration of hush-hush equipment. . . . The process is known to cynical Company hands as Carmelita's Dog and Pony Show, and it rarely fails. The recipient goes back to the Hill feeling like a real insider, and not only votes the Company more money and fewer restrictions, but tells the press what a fine job the CIA is doing. I wondered, not for the first time, what the Company was getting in return for this particular little rendezvous.

She pushed herself away from the trailer. "Well," she said, "I'm going to go change out of this bikini and take a nap. That call came too damn early this morning."

She paused, looking me up and down. "If you don't have any plans for dinner," she said, "you might like to come up to the house this evening, say about seven. No point in both of us eating alone."

"I'll be there," I said.

The weather continued to build up an attitude all through the long gray afternoon. By dinner time the sky was dark, the wind was full of spray and sand, and the big gray waves were piling onto the beach with a steady rolling crash as the sea clawed at the land. I tried not to think about the unstable pile of sand we were standing on, or the one hurricane I'd seen years ago on the coast of Mexico. For a man who knew more than most about the predictions of government agencies, I certainly was putting a lot of faith in the National Weather Service.

Standing at the foot of the steps, I paused and looked at the stack of plywood sheets I'd taken off the windows. If this got significantly worse than it was supposed to, some people were going to be wishing they'd left well enough alone. Serve the silly bastards right, I thought, and then laughed silently at myself. Turning into the grumpy caretaker already, was I?

Brenda opened the door before I could knock; she must have heard my feet on the sun deck. "Dane. Glad you came," she said, sounding as if she meant it. "This weather," she added as I stepped inside, "it gets on my nerves, you know? Being in this little place by myself, listening to that damn wind, I almost went down and asked you to come up ahead of time."

She had on a light-blue dress, cut loose—I don't know the term—and held at the waist by a silver chain. The skirt stopped a few inches above her knees; she appeared to be wearing hose. I wished I'd worn something a little more formal than jeans and T-shirt. At least I'd remembered to shave.

"Want a drink?" she said.

"Sure. Jim Beam," I said as she stepped behind the tiny bar, and then, "No, wait, I already took that down to the trailer . . . any decent bourbon, then."

She was peering under the bar. "Wild Turkey?"

"Outstanding. Straight up."

She poured a good healthy wallop and handed me the glass. "Sit down," she said. "A couple of things aren't done yet."

I let myself down on the couch. "Smoke if you want," she added. "It doesn't bother me."

"I don't smoke." I sipped at the Wild Turkey. Whatever the Company's other shortcomings, whoever had stocked the bar had known his business. "You go ahead, if you do."

She shook her head. "Jerry got me to quit. I don't know how much longer I'm going to hold out, though, if these uptight assholes don't quit getting in everybody's face about it. Seems like every time you turn around nowadays, they're preaching at you about something—don't smoke, don't drink, don't eat meat or anything else that tastes good, wear rubbers or better yet don't fuck at all. Jesus." She made a face. "I told Jerry the other day, why doesn't he introduce an amendment to the Constitution that says everybody has to mind their own damn business?"

She cocked her head, listening. "Boy, that wind, though, I could use a smoke right now. None on the island, though?" I shook my head. "Just as well, I guess . . . somebody talk you into quitting?"

"Never started. And I'm really not sure why." Most people start when they're teenagers, because the kids they hang out with all do it; and I hadn't hung out with anybody as a teenager, had spent most of my free time out in the woods alone with a gun or just riding around on a series of worn-out motorcycles. But I didn't want to talk about my socially maladjusted youth with Brenda. I finished my drink and set the glass down on the little coffee table.

"Refill?" Brenda said. "No? I better go check on dinner."

Dinner, when she finally called me in, consisted of something with breast of chicken and wild rice and some sort of sauce. It wasn't bad; it wouldn't have won any prizes, but it was considerably better than I'd expected. I wouldn't have figured Brenda for the domestic type. I said, "Well, you can cook."

She laughed. "I can? What do you think that is? E-Zee Gourmet Frozen Dinners, you dummy, cooked to perfection in their own little cardboard boxes and served artistically to look like the real thing. I cannot tell a lie, I did it with my little microwave. . . . what the hell did you expect, Dane? Where would I get the stuff to fix something like that here, even if I had any idea how? This is just some of the stuff that old Indian brought out."

I said, "I'll be damned. But it's pretty good, for frozen food."

She shrugged. "Well, I did fool with it a little bit, added a sprinkle or two of this and that—I do know how to cook," she said, "a little anyway, though I hate doing it. I was raised by an old aunt who made me learn these ladylike skills."

She refilled her glass from the wine bottle that stood in the center of the table. Her knuckles were white. "My God, listen to that wind," she muttered. "Are you sure we're safe?"

"No," I said. She looked at me with widening eyes and I added, "But I don't think there's much danger from this storm, if that's what you mean."

"Well, I hate it." She gulped her wine. "I'm a city girl, Dane. Grew up in Philadelphia, lived in the D.C. area since I got old enough to leave home. I don't care for all this island business, nothing but sand and water and those damn birds squawking all the time. A beach is fine, but give me a first-class resort hotel right behind it with a good night club or at least a piano lounge."

"So why did you come?"

"It's what Jerry wanted to do. And the customer is always right," she said, giving me a slightly belligerent look. "Hadn't you heard?"

I didn't respond. After a moment she said in a quieter voice, "Anyway, we can't be seen together in public places, especially not now. Jerry's in a certain amount of shit back home. Got this bunch of religious fanatics running around trying to get him defeated in next year's elections because he didn't go quite as far as they wanted on the abortion thing. You figure what they could do with a scandal right now, especially as popular as his wife is."

She fell silent, staring into her glass, while I finished my food. I noticed she hadn't eaten much.

"Leave everything," she said as I stood up. "I'll clean up tomorrow . . . damn, I wish I had a cigarette." She went back into the front room and I followed. "Don't go yet," she said, sitting down in one of the wicker chairs. "Want another drink or anything? See if that radio will get anything."

It wouldn't; as I'd expected, the storm was screwing the reception along the coast. There were chopped-up bars of music, isolated fragments of human speech, but nothing coherent, only hiss and crackle and whine. By now the storm outside was in full cry. Sheets of hard-driven rain slammed against the windows. Brenda shivered and folded her legs under her. There was a sheen that wasn't skin; she was wearing stockings, all right.

I said, "I guess I'd better get back to the trailer pretty soon." I didn't sound very sincere, even to myself. "Thanks for dinner."

She stood up. "Bull *shit* you will," she said flatly, moving toward the bar. "No way in *hell* are you going to leave me here alone to sit out this damn storm."

She went behind the bar and grabbed a bottle and poured herself a very large drink. I couldn't see the label from where I sat, but I had the impression she'd just gone for the first bottle that came handy.

I said, "Well, fine, I'll stay awhile longer. If that's what you want."

Dane, you silver-tongued devil. I wondered what the hell was wrong with me. But this wasn't at all my usual sort of scene.

She came out from behind the bar, holding the bottle in one hand and the glass in the other. She walked to the center of the room and stood facing me, feet apart.

"What I want," she said, "what I thought we'd do, since there's not a lot else to do around here—" She waved toward the doorway behind her with the hand that held the glass. "I thought we might go into the bedroom and take our clothes off and more or less fuck our brains out for awhile. Would you like to do that?"

That, I thought as I followed her into the darkened bedroom, must be what they mean by making an offer you can't refuse. . . .

In the bedroom she flipped on a dresser-top lamp and I sat down on the edge of the bed and got undressed. She came over and stood in front of me, watching me. "All right," she said approvingly.

She undid a clasp and laid the silver chain on top of the dresser. Bending down, her eyes still watching me watching her, she took hold of the skirt and pulled the blue dress up and over her head in a single smooth motion, not teasing me with it but not hurrying either. Underneath she was wearing tiny cream-colored panties and a matching bra that didn't look quite up to the job it was having to do. There was a fair bit of lace in evidence, and a few little bows. She had on sheer stockings, not pantyhose, with a skimpy garter belt that matched the rest of the outfit. She struck a pose, turning slightly, one knee bent, hip out, hands behind head: corny, but effective. "Like it?"

I didn't speak; she didn't really seem to expect an answer. "I knew you would," she said, reaching back to unhook the bra. "You tough guys are all romantics at heart, go for that lacy-pretty look. It's mostly the little wimps who have to have all that mean-looking black stuff, spiked heels and leather and all, before they can get it up."

She bent to slide her panties down over her hips, the narrow white straps of the garters coming taut over the curve of her buttocks. I said, "How do you know I'm a tough guy?"

She straightened, kicked off her shoes, and reached out and pushed me back onto the bed. She climbed on top of me, straddling me on her knees.

"Well," she said, reaching for me, fitting herself to me, "I don't know how tough you are, but you're sure as hell hard. . . ."

Later—I don't know how much later; at the time, it seemed like quite awhile—I lay on my back and watched as she got out of bed and put one foot up on a chair and began undoing her garter-belt clasps. "All this stuff," she said, "it's a turnon when you're getting started—okay, it turns me on too, wearing it—but these damn stockings cost way too much to lie around in all night, getting runs. Anyway, it's not all that comfortable after awhile."

She rolled the stockings down and slipped them off, hanging them carefully over the back of the chair, and took off the garter belt and got back into bed naked. "Ah, that's better . . . what did I do with that bottle?"

"On the floor beside the bed, I think."

"Right, hang on. I'll get it." A gust of wind shook the house as she moved on all fours to reach across me, her big breasts dangling against my arm. I could see little blue veins under the pale skin. "Here we are," she said, straightening. "Want some?"

I took the bottle and looked at the label. Johnny Walker. As a Kentucky native I probably wasn't supposed to drink Scotch, but what the hell. I said, "As Jimmy Buffet said, if you're going to get blown away, you might as well get blown away. . . ." And took a long satisfying pull, while the rain blasted against the roof and walls, almost drowning out the bass rumble of the waves down on the beach.

She held out a hand. "Come on—" I handed her the bottle and the lights went out.

The shock was enough to paralyze us both for a moment, even though it should have been obvious that it could happen at any time in a storm like this. The darkness was almost absolute.

Brenda said distinctly, "Shit."

I said, "I don't suppose you know where there's a flashlight."

"I know where there's a candle," she said. "Feel around over on the top of the dresser, you'll find it. Stuck in a champagne bottle, and there ought to be some matches somewhere near it. We got into this thing with candlelight the other night."

I didn't ask her for details. I got up carefully and felt my way over to the dresser, almost tripping over one of Brenda's shoes. A little groping located the half-burned candle easily enough; the matches took a little longer. I got a match lit, finally, and touched it to the blackened wick. A soft yellowish light filled the room.

I said, "I can't work on the electricity until morning. If the storm's over then. Could be a line down, could be something wrong with the generator, might just be a fuse."

"It's all right." She stretched out, wriggling slightly, as I got back into bed. "In this light you won't be able to see my big butt as well."

"Looks okay to me. Feels okay, too—"

"Oh, horse shit, Dane. I could lose ten, twenty pounds and look a hundred percent better, and you damn well know it. I'm twenty-seven years old," she said. It was a couple of years under my own estimate, but credible enough. "All this big jiggly stuff that you guys like so much, pretty soon it's all going to start heading south, you know? You wouldn't believe how fast a woman with this kind of shape can go from bounce to floop. And my butt *is* too big."

She sat up, holding the Johnny Walker bottle. "Look, Dane," she said, "I know what I've got and what I haven't got. I may have made some bad mistakes in my life, but I haven't gone in for bullshitting myself in a lot of years. . . . Tell you something else, big guy, I'm not even in the same class with Jerry's wife. You ever see her?"

"Pictures in magazines."

"Yeah, well, I've seen pictures you haven't. Jerry showed me some Polaroids he took a couple of years ago when they'd both had a few, her in her bikini by their pool, and believe me, she's still in great shape. She could walk in here right now and take off her clothes and you wouldn't look back at me." She laughed. "And she's at least ten years older than me. Don't know how the hell she does it."

She rolled over on her stomach and grinned at me. "Which probably makes you wonder why he's running around risking everything for a few rolls with me when he's got something better at home."

I said, "Well, technique is more important than equipment—"

"You're sweet. Just a tiny bit scary, but sweet. But no, it's a lot simpler than that. Some guys like black lingerie, some guys like blow jobs, some guys get it up for other guys. Guys like Jerry, their big turnon is getting away with something. Risking everything? That's the point of the whole thing."

"I'll be damned." I thought about it. You ran into men like that in my line of work, from time to time. Most of them eventually took one risk too many and were never heard from again, but a few made a life of it. I'd wondered sometimes if that might not be part of what went into making a double agent: the extra rush of knowing you were playing with disaster in two directions at once. Something else occurred to me and I said, "He showed you pictures of his wife in a bikini?"

"Oh, Jerry's got his little quirks. You'd be surprised how strange his kicks get sometimes. That's one thing I'm enjoying about tonight, Dane—being with a man who doesn't need funny stuff. It gets tiring after awhile."

She took a drink and set the bottle carefully on the floor. "You have to understand," she said, "there's no bullshit going on between Jerry and me. I mean, he's not giving me any line about wanting to leave her for me, and I wouldn't be stupid enough to believe it if he did. We're not in love or anything like that. In our own ways, we're both in this for what we can get out of it."

"Which is?" I didn't really give a damn but she obviously wanted to talk about it. "What do you get out of it?"

She turned onto her side and leaned on her elbow. "You know what Madonna says. I'm a material girl."

She squirmed over closer to me. Her hand began tracing lines across my back. "Christ, you've got some scars back here. From the war?"

"From a war." I ran my own hand along her flank. "Of sorts."

"I'll bet. I'll bet you could tell some stories. But you're not going to, are you? Boy, you play your cards close to your chest, anybody ever tell you that?" She started fiddling with my hair. "I don't even know your first name."

"Randall."

"Randall? Randall Dane. Hm." She reached down and took my hand and put it on her breast. "Right there, do you mind? Yes, do that . . . Randy?"

"Don't even think it."

"Okay, okay. What the hell do they call you, then?"

"Dane." I shook my head. "That's all anybody ever calls me. Just Dane." Last time anybody called me anything else, they called me Sergeant; and that was long ago, in a galaxy far away.

Brenda said, "Are you married, Dane?"

"No."

"Ever been?"

"Yes."

"Divorced?"

"She died."

"Oh." Her voice was suddenly very small. "I'm sorry."

"It's all right." It wasn't, but I didn't want to listen to apologies. "Let it go."

I took the bottle and hit myself with a hard one. "To answer what you were working up to, though," I said, "she called me Dane too."

For a few minutes neither of us spoke. Outside the storm was ranting and screeching across the island, the surf and the thunder joining in a tremendous barrage of sound. The candle was beginning to burn low.

"Lie down," she said at last. "Let me do something now."

I lay there as her lips worked their way down my chest and stomach, little moist butterfly contacts. She took me in hand and lowered her face toward me, browsing and nibbling and then suddenly taking me in, while I grasped the back of her head with both hands and fought for control.

After a few minutes she raised her head and looked at me. "Feel like the real thing?"

I nodded. She rolled over and got onto all fours, elbows braced on the pillow, her wide fine bottom glowing softly in the candlelight. As I went in she made a low guttural sound, half growl and half purr, pushing herself back against me. "Dane," she muttered. "Come on, Dane—"

At the moment of climax she bucked hard and then collapsed forward, breasts flattening against the pillow, while I sank down on top of her. "Yes," was all she said, and she said it very quietly.

Outside the wind rose in a demented scream.

8

•••••

WEDNESDAY MORNING CAMERON CALLED.

"You having radio trouble again?" he wanted to know. "I been trying to reach you since eight."

I said, "We had a power failure during the storm. I got the electricity working again, but the RT's been even crazier than before. Can lightning do that?"

"How the hell would I know? That particular set, anything's possible." His voice was faint, the connection weak and unsteady. "Your, uh, guest, you know? He couldn't get through to you at all. Finally called me up."

"I'm surprised you ever made it. And I don't seem to be able to call out at all from here. For God's sake," I said crankily, "get somebody down here to fix this lousy ship-to-shore. Or island-to-shore. Whatever."

Cameron said, "I'll work on it. Meanwhile the main man said tell you he's on his way back. Called me from the Houston airport, so it shouldn't be long. You know the routine by now."

"Meet him at the dock and make sure Harry Reasoner and Barbara Walters aren't lurking in the shadows with camera crews."

"You got the general idea, son. Everything okay? No major storm damage?"

"Nothing I haven't already fixed. Except—"

"The RT, yeah. Okay—" He said something else that I couldn't understand; the phone went dead. I figured it didn't matter.

Brenda came in off the sun deck, glistening all over with suntan lotion. She wasn't even bothering with the bikini now. I said, "You're going to have a really interesting sunburn if you don't watch it."

"So I'm watching it. Got enough of this crap on me to float a submarine. . . . You should have seen Jerry," she said, "smearing on the sunblock, covering everything up, hugging the shade, because it might raise some questions if he showed up back in D.C. with a fresh tan. Speaking of Jerry," she added, "was that him just now?"

"Somebody else calling for him. He's on his way." I replaced the phone in its cradle, resisting an impulse to hit the set repeatedly with the handiest blunt instrument. All these supertech spook gadgets, they could eavesdrop on a conversation in a building across the street or intercept Soviet missile-tracking transmissions from halfway around the world, but they couldn't provide a simple ship-to-shore telephone that worked properly. Typical Company effort; half the weekend pleasure-boat owners along the coast had better equipment.

I said, "I better get my things and head back for the mainland. I'm supposed to meet him at the dock."

She stood there in the doorway naked, looking me up and down. "I guess we've got time for one more," she said. "You want to? Just for the hell of it?"

I thought about it. "I don't think so."

She nodded. "Me neither. Might be fun, but that's just a little bit sleazy even for me. I better get something on, then."

But she didn't move; she continued to stand there looking

at me. "If you're wondering," she said, "I'm not going to tell him."

"Don't you think he'll know? I think I would." I wondered, now I heard myself say it. No doubt every man thinks he'd know, but who can ever be sure?

"I don't really know," she said. "Even if he suspects, though, he won't say anything about it. To either of us."

"Broad-minded type." ·

"Not that. It would just create too many ego problems if he admitted to himself that I do it with other guys. He sort of needs to pretend to himself that he owns me."

She laughed. "You never know about Jerry, though. He just might get some kind of weird kick out of the idea of sharing me with a CIA spook. Anyway, don't worry about it."

"I wasn't worrying."

"You weren't, were you? Even though you must have some idea how many ways he could find to make life hell for you, with his connections . . . I said the other night that you were a little bit scary, Dane. I've just figured out why," she said, putting her hands on her bare hips. "You just don't give a damn, do you? Nothing really gets to you."

There was nothing at all to say to that. At least I couldn't think of anything. I went out the door, hearing her laugh as I went down the redwood steps.

I didn't have to wait long at the dock before the gray car appeared up the road. The sun was just going over the top of its arc. Raintree must have driven pretty fast; I wondered if he'd considered the possible consequences of getting ticketed, or even stopped, down here.

He pulled into the gravel lot and jumped out of the car, giving me the big photo-opportunity smile. He still had the jackass cap and the mirror shades. "Hey," he said genially.

"Good to see you're all right. Is Brenda okay too?"

I nodded and he said, "Good. I was worried when I heard there'd been a storm, and then I couldn't reach you. Came pretty close to renting a seaplane or a chopper at Houston and flying down. No major damage?"

"Only the RT, and it didn't work very well to begin with."

"Fine. Fine." He rubbed his palms together briskly. "God, it feels good to be back down here, away from all that craziness on the Hill. Just smell that sea air."

He got his little nylon bag from the front seat and locked the car doors. I said, "How did your business go? The big vote you had to be there for?"

He looked surprised. "You didn't hear? On the news?"

"The radio wasn't working very well," I said. "The weather."

I couldn't very well tell him that I didn't even know what his bill was about, and didn't give a damn either, and hadn't been listening to the radio anyway because I was busy screwing his girl friend. He might have taken offense.

He said, "Well, we won. Close, but we stopped the bastards cold." He might have been Crazy Horse reporting to Sitting Bull that Custer had just been fitted for his Arrow shirt; the famous grin was now distinctly predatory. "Man," he said, "winning really gets the juices flowing."

As we walked toward the dock I said, "You seem to be in a good mood. Last time I saw you, you were telling me how none of this made any difference."

"Oh, well, you know, you get in these moods sometimes. Just goes with the job . . . of course it probably *doesn't* make any difference," he added, "but what the hell, that's not the point anyway, is it?"

"Then what is?"

"Why, the *rush*, Dane, don't you know that?" We stopped at the end of the dock and he swung around to look up at me. "But then you don't know, do you? Nobody does, who hasn't been part of it. It's the most exciting game in the world. Anybody who tells you he's in it for any other reason, he's either lying or in it for what he can steal. Or he's a dangerous fanatic."

As he started to climb down into the skiff I said, "If you need me for anything and you can't get that damn RT to work, get the shotgun and fire a couple of rounds. I probably won't hear you up at the motel, but Billy Jumper hears everything, and he'll come get me."

He jumped down into the skiff. "Thanks," he said. "I doubt if I'll be calling on you, though." He gave me a suggestive leer. "I think I'm going to be making up for lost time, you know?"

I watched him motor off across the bay until he was just a dark spot against the sunlit water; then I picked up my duffel bag and started walking once again toward the Bayport Motel. I hoped they'd fixed the sports channel by now. I wasn't up to listening to any discussions about sex today.

In the evening, just as the sun was going down, I walked across the road to the little store and bought a couple of pieces of extremely bad fried chicken and a stale roll from their ready-to-eat counter. They had a couple of formica tables in back and I sat and chewed the chicken and washed it down with a Coke. It needed all the washing down I could give it.

I bought a Houston newspaper from the rack by the cash register and tried to find out what Raintree had been doing in Washington; all right, he'd gotten me curious in spite of myself. I didn't have much luck. There were plenty of quotes from people on both sides of yesterday's wrangle, the winners hailing the vote as a victory for responsible government and the losers muttering darkly that this wasn't over yet; there was even an editorial deploring the results. But I still couldn't figure out what the bill had been about. Something to do with capital gains; since I had no capital and hardly any gains lately, I decided it couldn't affect me.

There was a photo of Raintree, though, posing with several other bright stars of the winning faction. They all seemed to be trying out for the Olympic smiling team. Representative Jerry Raintree, the article said, had flown back from a fact-finding visit to secret intelligence bases, location unspecified, to lead his party's efforts.

The President had declined comment.

Not much else seemed to be happening at home or abroad. There were brush fires in the Southwest, tornadoes in the Midwest, and a new serial killer in New York City. A tribe of Indians had lost a court suit to stop mining on their sacred burial grounds. There were fresh riots in Jerusalem. In Lebanon, a Muslim extremist group had put out a warning that the holy war would soon be carried to the Americans in new ways; the State Department downplayed the threat, but there were plans to beef up security at airports just in case.

I tossed the paper onto the table, finished the Coke, and got up and left the store. It was dark outside by now; huge insects splattered themselves against the store's front window below the sign that read FOOD—GAS. Surely a rare case of truth in advertising; I was already wishing I'd bought a pack of Alka-Seltzer before leaving.

I started back across the road toward the motel. A familiar pickup truck grunted to a stop beside me and Billy Jumper said, "Back with us again, eh?"

I leaned against the dented fender. "Looks like it," I said. "The man came back."

"Thought I saw him heading across in the skiff. Wasn't handling it well enough to be you. . . . Been out on the water all day," he said, "didn't catch hardly anything. Guess they're still nervous from the storm."

He rested his arms on the wheel and looked at me. In the dim light he appeared to be wearing an amused expression, as if he wanted to laugh but was holding it in. "Stayed kind of busy out there the last couple of days, didn't you?" he said. "I went past yesterday a couple of times, close enough to throw rocks ashore, and you weren't in sight."

I said, "I had to fix a few things."

"Uh huh. I just bet you did," he said drily. "I bet you were so busy with your fixing, you didn't even see the plane."

"Plane?"

"That blue seaplane I told you about last week, remember? It flew over, late yesterday afternoon, going slow. Went right across the bay, south to north, and then headed out to sea. Same plane, or one just like it."

"Hm." I didn't ask him if he was sure. "No, you're right, I missed the whole thing. I was out back fooling with the generator about that time, wouldn't have heard anything with that diesel running."

I wondered what was going on. Have to call Cameron up in the morning, let him worry about it. Maybe now he'd take a little interest.

"Saw one of those funny inflatable motorboats today, too," he said. "Didn't get a good look at it, it was a long way off, but I'm pretty sure that's what it was."

He shook his head. "Sure getting to be a busy place lately," he mused. "Looks like—"

He stopped, turning his head slowly. I said, "What,"

and he held up a hand. After a moment he said, "Huh. Hear that?"

I couldn't hear anything but the wind and the hum of the store's ice machine and the rattle of a motel-room air conditioner.

"Out on the bay," Billy Jumper added. "Couple of good-sized motors."

I heard it then, the rumble of distant exhausts, growing steadily louder. Somebody was moving pretty fast for a moonless night like this; after a storm there would be big pieces of driftwood and other junk in the channel for days, ugly stuff to run into at full throttle in the dark.

"Sounds like they're heading toward the island," Billy said. "Don't reckon Ray and his buddies might be going out to raise some hell, do you? Could be trouble if they do, what with the Congressman and his lady out there. . . ."

I listened to the growing double drone, wondering. They did seem to be moving in that direction. Of course there was nothing unusual in that; the island was right in the middle of the inshore channel, and dozens of powerboats passed nearby on any average day, fishing or towing waterskiers or just screwing around. Still—

I said, "Oh, my God."

"What's the matter?"

"Wait here," I said. "Please."

I ran across the road toward the motel, cursing under my breath. It had finally come to me what was happening; I saw the whole thing in terrible detail. Later I might spend some time kicking my own ass for not seeing it sooner; right now there was no time to waste on that. There might be no time at all.

The key stuck in the lock and I jiggled it frantically, kicking at the door, before it finally came open. I dived for the dresser, grabbed up the .44, and was back out the door, running hard toward the pickup.

Billy Jumper had the engine running already. "Dock?" he said as I piled into the cab beside him.

"Yes. And go like hell."

He gunned the old engine, spraying gravel, and we roared down the half-mile stretch of road to the boat dock. He didn't ask questions. I sat clutching the .44, refusing to let myself think about what I was going to do, what I was almost certainly going to be up against with nothing but a Civil War horse pistol. I only hoped I wouldn't be too late to do anything at all.

He hit the brakes and I jumped out before the pickup stopped moving. "I'm taking your boat," I shouted over my shoulder as I ran for the dock.

"Motor's still warm," he called after me. "I just came in a little while ago. Don't choke it or you'll flood it."

The old Johnson bucked and sputtered and died when I cranked it; I yanked the starter rope again and then once more before it caught. I twisted the throttle viciously and the boat rose up on its tail like a wheeling motorcycle and charged out into the night.

There was no moon but the sky was clear, all the clouds long blown away. The starlight was very bright, flashing off the wavetops in little silver splinters of light. Out ahead, a single yellow light marked the location of the island; thank God they hadn't turned the lights off yet. I looked in all directions for the running lights of other boats—this was no time to get myself run down, running without any lights of my own—but there was nothing.

With the outboard in full blare I couldn't hear the motors I'd heard from the mainland; that was all right as long as they couldn't hear me either. I didn't try to look for them. The Zodiacs would be impossible to spot—lying low in the water, they wouldn't show up well even in the daylight; it's one reason for their popularity in certain circles. And it was a sure thing *they* wouldn't be showing any lights, not now. Afterward, they'd have some sort of signal . . . but I yanked my mind away from the thought of afterward.

The water was rough; the old flat-bottomed boat slammed hard over the wave crests and boomed as it hit the troughs, rearing up under the outboard's thrust, rocking dangerously as it angled across the wave pattern. The island was dead ahead now, the light resolving itself into a rectangle of window hanging above the dark shape of the island itself. I pushed the throttle bar over, swinging the bow through a few degrees' arc, trying to form a mental picture of the shoreline on this side of the island.

As the black bulk of the island rose up against the starlit water, I cut power to the motor, easing down to little more than trolling speed, the big Johnson making no more than a soft deep burble now. Everything inside my skin was screaming to gas the damn thing, this was no time to be slowing down; but I still couldn't hear the other motors, and if they were already ashore and heard me coming I was dead and so was everyone else.

I could see the beach now, the wet sand along the water's edge shining in the starlight. Turning the boat sharply, praying that the sound of the waves on the windward side of the island would mask the sound of the Johnson, I opened the throttle slightly and drove straight toward the beach. As the squared-off metal bow slid up into the shallows, I killed the outboard and tilted it upward, letting the boat's momentum carry it hard aground. There was a swish and a soft grinding sound of sand against metal and the boat stopped.

I was already jumping over the bow and running down the beach, staying close to the water's edge where the sand was wet and firm and I could run faster. It was also more exposed out there, but if anyone was looking this way it was all over anyway. The light continued to shine in the house, casting a pale glow through the live-oaks; I'd landed almost exactly where I'd planned, a hundred yards or so from the house, where the point and the live-oaks masked my approach. I couldn't hear anything yet except the surf on the far side of the island.

The soft sand dragged at my feet and slowed me as I cut across the beach and scuttled up the face of a dune, the tall grasses slapping at my legs. I held the .44 high, hoping no sand had gotten into the antiquated action. I was behind the house now, moving up fast, seeing the silver shine of the trailer just ahead. From the blockhouse came the steady thump of the power-plant diesel, just loud enough to cover any sounds I might be making.

And now I could hear what I'd been listening for: the muted grumble of a pair of idling motors, somewhere down near the dock. . . .

I had meant to get to the house and warn Raintree and Brenda, get my hands on that shotgun and turn on the floodlights around the sun deck and wait for the bastards—and put Raintree on that damn radiotelephone, see if he could get off a call for help. It wasn't going to happen that way. As I came out from behind the trailer I saw immediately that it was too late.

I spotted four of them at first. One was at the foot of the steps, starting to climb, his head turned, apparently about to say something to the man coming across the sand right behind him. Two more were coming up the walkway from the dock, side by side. They all carried weapons; it was too dark to identify hardware, or to make out details of how they were dressed.

Then another man came up the walkway, and I heard the sound of feet on the boards behind him. Time was up; let the games begin.

I thumbed back the hammer of the Dragoon pistol and shot the nearest man off the steps. The black-powder load made an amazingly long bright flame in the darkness. The man threw his hands up, still clutching his weapon—some sort of automatic rifle, I thought—and pitched backward onto the sand.

The man behind him jumped back just as I fired again. I dived into the shadow of the pilings beneath the house, steadying the big .44 against a piling, and banged off a third soft-lead ball at the men on the walkway, who were just starting to get unstuck. One of them went down; I couldn't tell how seriously I'd hit him.

Voices were screaming back and forth now, curses and frantic questions in Arabic, and what sounded like a cry of pain. They were all hitting the deck, diving for whatever cover there was, even though they still didn't seem to be sure where the fire was coming from. No doubt about it: whoever they were, they'd been shot at before, and more than once. They had the reactions of old infantrymen. I touched off one more shot at a dim crawling shape and ducked behind the piling as the darkness exploded in automatic fire.

Overhead, in the house, the light went out. I thought I could hear Brenda screaming.

A burst of bullets chewed splinters from the pilings a couple of feet from my face. I rolled to one side and crawled, fast as I could manage in the soft sand, while more bullets searched among the pilings for me. I heard the plunk of stray shots hitting the redwood planks overhead, and hoped to God those two had sense enough to lie flat and stay still.

A voice cried in Arabic, "Don't shoot at the house! We don't want to kill him!"

That was interesting, if I'd had time to think about it,

but I didn't. I started to fire at a nearby muzzle flash and remembered in time that I only had two shots left. I might be able to make it to the storeroom, where the powder was stashed, but there was no chance of reloading the Dragoon gun in time to do any good. I lay still and watched and waited while the attackers got it together and made their play.

They weren't amateurs; they were spreading out in opposite directions to flank and finally surround the house, one man running while the others laid down covering fire. It was very good tactics; I wondered what the hell I was going to do about it. . . .

They could have gotten me if they'd had a little more patience; all they had to do was complete their flanking movement and then smoke me out with a crossfire. But I hadn't returned fire or shown myself, and maybe somebody decided I was already dead—or out of ammunition, which was almost true. A voice yelled in Arabic, "We have no time for this!" and somebody answered with something I didn't catch.

And suddenly here they came, two of them, dashing across the open space in front of the house, coming toward me, firing from the hip, while covering fire spattered among the pilings. I heard a wild shout of "*Al-hamdulillah!*" as the nearest one charged in; I cocked the .44 and steadied down on the shadowy running figure in the starlight—

Directly overhead, there was a sudden loud hollow boom, followed instantly by a metallic racking sound, a muffled clang, and then another boom. A geyser of sand erupted between the two running men.

The man bringing up the rear didn't wait to analyze the situation; he leaped into the cover of a live-oak as a third shot kicked up sand where he had been. The nearer one seemed momentarily baffled. He turned half around and looked upward, his weapon's muzzle poking uncertainly here and there.

I shot him before he could recover, then shot him again as he staggered and swung back around toward me. As he fell I slid out from between the pilings and grabbed his weapon, hearing the sphincter-puckering pop of bullets coming entirely too close. Sand sprayed across my legs from a near-miss; splinters hit my back as I scrambled back into the cover of the pilings. Up on the deck the shotgun fired again.

And thank you, Congressman Raintree. Thank you very much indeed for that contribution to this evening's symposium. . . .

Even in the dark my hands recognized the shape of an AK-47. Somehow I wasn't surprised. The long selector lever on the right side of the receiver was set on full-automatic, which was fine with me. The odds were still terrible, but they'd just gotten a lot better.

I snapped off a short burst in the general direction of the last set of muzzle flashes, the AK-47 bucking and kicking satisfyingly in my hands. There was an instant's pause as the attackers absorbed the implications of this development; but then they opened up again, returning my fire with interest. I wondered how many rounds were left in this piece. The guy had been doing a lot of shooting.

There was a shout from down by the boat dock. The attackers stopped firing for a moment and I recognized the voice of the man called Ali, bellowing in Arabic: "Back to the boats! Back to the boats! Time to get out of here!"

Other voices rose in argument, but Ali wasn't having any of it. "In the name of God, back to the boats!" he yelled. "It's all over, you fools. And more of the devils are on their way."

In the distance I heard the sound of a boat coming from

the mainland, something big and running full out. Over the note of the motor came the tomcat wail of a siren.

I could hear feet moving back down toward the dock. I stayed where I was; they could go with my blessing. Down by the dock a motor burst into full roar, then another.

I got to my feet and moved slowly out from beneath the house. In a few minutes I could hear the two Zodiacs blasting southward down the inshore channel.

I looked up toward the house. Raintree's voice called down. "Is it all right to turn the light on?"

He sounded shaky. I didn't blame him. I said, "I don't see why not."

The floodlights around the deck came on, blinding me for a moment; I squinted and put my hand up to my eyes. When I could see again, Raintree was standing at the top of the steps, still holding the shotgun, looking down at me. All he had on was a pair of low-cut black briefs.

"Jesus Christ," he said blankly. "What the hell was that all about?"

I said, "Is Brenda all right?"

"Brenda? Oh, yes." There was an indistinct voice from inside, and Raintree said, "She says she's fine. I had her lie down on the floor when the shooting started."

The motor and the siren were getting close. I walked down to the boat dock as the siren died away. A powerful spotlight was probing along the shoreline.

A voice called, "You all right, Dane?"

Billy Jumper switched off the spotlight and I saw that he was standing at the wheel of a big, fast-looking powerboat. There appeared to be some sort of official insignia on the bows.

"Figured you might need some help," he said. "This boat belongs to the game warden, he keeps it at my dock. Thought maybe it might scare the bad guys a little bit if they heard me coming. My," he said admiringly, "got a nice loud sireen on this thing. Never ran one before. Everything under control out here? I heard those two Zodiacs leaving."

I said, "It's all right now."

"Then I better get this rig back to where I got it. Don't think I'll get in any real trouble for borrowing it, but I'd hate to lose that county contract and the dock fees."

I climbed tiredly back up to the house as he motored off. I was still carrying the AK-47. There was no reason for that; I leaned it against a piling and then went poking under the house until I found the .44 where I'd dropped it. I shoved it into my belt, feeling a certain affection for the ridiculous weapon; it had done its job tonight.

Raintree was standing at the foot of the steps, staring down at the body of the first man I'd killed. The floodlights revealed a short, chunky figure in jeans and a long-sleeved black pullover shirt. His face was blackened. He might have been twenty years old, not much more. The smell said that he had filled his trousers as his final revolutionary act.

I said, "Well, Congressman, that's what I call a meaningful fucking dialogue."

9

•••••

CAMERON SAID, "I HEARD YOU WERE GOOD. I didn't know you were this good."

He took off his hat and rubbed his scalp. "Or you could read the word 'crazy' in there. As in I heard you were crazy but I didn't know you were this crazy."

He dug a pack of cigarettes out of his shirt pocket and tapped one out and stuck it in his mouth. "Wife got me to quit these things a month ago," he said. "Now you've gone and got me to start again. Jesus *Christ*, Dane. You take on, what, eight to ten of these bastards?"

"I don't really know. Counting a couple staying with the boats, that's probably about right."

Cameron shook his head and thumbed a plastic throw-away lighter. "All of them," he said, puffing, "armed with automatic weapons, and all of them obviously experienced commando types—and you take them on with a damn pistol. And not even a decent pistol, but a fucking black powder hogleg that ought to be hanging on a museum wall, for God's sake."

I said, "Well, what would you have had me do?"

"Oh, don't misunderstand, Dane. I'm *glad* you're so many bricks shy of a load. If you were playing with a full deck the shit would really be hitting the fan about now. Bad enough when this kind of thing happens in Lebanon or Palestine. On U.S. soil, and to a serving Congressman as well, oh my bleeding ass. . . ." He shuddered. "Any time you find yourself in a similar situation, you got my blessing to do the same thing. Take on the whole *world* by yourself."

"I wasn't entirely on my own," I pointed out. "Raintree got into it with the shotgun."

Cameron snorted. "And, as far as we can tell, didn't hit a damn thing."

"Maybe not," I said, "although some of those guys may be somewhere bleeding to death right now from shot wounds, for all we know. But it doesn't matter. He created a diversion when I needed one—and," I added, "when a lot of men would have been hiding under the bed."

"Yeah, you're right. Guy did show a lot of guts, more than I'd have given him credit for. I shouldn't make cracks. . . ." Cameron threw his cigarette down half-smoked. "Don't mind me. This is just such a damn mess."

He turned and leaned against the redwood railing and looked down at the busy scene below. We were standing on the sun deck; it seemed to be the only place on this end of the island where we could stay out of the way of the Company tech team that was systematically going over the ground of last night's fire fight. They looked like cops checking out the scene of a crime for evidence, and in a sense that was what was going on; all they needed was a couple of chalk outlines where the bodies had fallen, though it might have been hard to mark on sand. The two deceased gunmen, however, had already left the island in a couple of body bags, in the custody of more Company hands. All in all an efficient operation; I might have been impressed if I hadn't been up all night and now most of the day as well.

"Had some problems over on the mainland last night, did you?" Cameron said.

"When I went over to use Billy's phone," I said, "after I finally gave up trying to get through to you on that lousy RT. Hell, I already told you the whole story."

It had been quite a little confrontation. The gunfire had drawn the interest of a young and very green county-mountie who had been driving through, probably looking for teenage drunks and other threats to Western civilization. He'd cut me off as I came off the dock, backed me up against the wall of the boat shed, and shouted a series of questions that made no sense even if I'd been inclined to answer them. He was obviously out of his depth and on the edge of panic. He kept pointing his shiny new chrome-plated revolver at me, holding it in a two-hand death grip, the muzzle wavering all over Texas, and I'd thought for a bit there that I was going to have to take it away from him to keep from getting shot.

No doubt we made quite a little tableau, standing there at the end of the pavement in the flashing blue-and-white lights, yelling at each other; probably gave the few residents of Bayport something to talk about for months, if they didn't sleep through the whole thing. Finally I managed to convince the damn fool to call up the sheriff in Soto. I couldn't hear any of the conversation, but his boss must have chewed him several new body orifices when he finally got him on the horn. The kid came away from the car practically prepared to kiss my butt, and wasted even more of my time assuring me there wouldn't be any further trouble.

It should have been no big deal for me, with all my years of dealing with Third World cops—Christ, I was in Uganda right after Idi Amin left, with drunk soldiers running wild all over the country, stopping people at random and now and then shooting somebody for no reason beyond casual impulse. But just then, this had been something I didn't need; that poor deputy couldn't possibly have known how close to the edge I was.

I said, "You were right about having the local law trained."

"Texas," Cameron said. "Well, it's all under control now, everything swept neatly under the good old national-security rug. In the highly unlikely event that anybody gets inquisitive, what happened last night was a training exercise carried out by a special secret counter-terrorist team."

"Do tell. That little shuffle this morning, with the chopper, was that national security too?"

Before the day was more than a pale line over the eastern horizon, Jerry Raintree and his companion had become less than a memory as far as this island was concerned. The helicopter had landed as soon as Cameron's men were satisfied the island was secure, and taken off again just as quickly as Raintree and Brenda could be hustled aboard. A second chopper had patrolled the area around the island to make sure no boats came near.

Cameron said, "Of course it's a matter of national security, Dane. What could be more damaging to the security of the U.S. of A. than to have people losing faith in the moral stature of their elected leaders? Especially," he added with a straight face, "when we're talking about leaders who routinely vote the right way on intelligence and security matters . . . too bad there's no way to tell the voters about that cowboy routine with the shotgun, without telling them the rest of it. Probably be good for a few votes next year."

A man came up the steps, carrying a clipboard. Cameron said, "You tech wienies going to be much longer, Leonard?"

Leonard was looking over his notes. He was a thin, pale-faced guy about my age with a long nose and rimless glasses. "We haven't got much," he admitted. "Two bodies,

Mediterranean-type males, evidently early twenties, no identification of any kind, no papers on them. Blood in a couple
of other places—"

"I'm fairly sure I hit at least one more of them," I
said.

"Oh?" He made a notation on his pad. "Badly enough
that he might have to be taken to a doctor somewhere?"

"Damn if I know. Those soft-lead .44 balls must make a
hell of a wound, but it couldn't have been too bad, because
they all left under their own power. Nobody carrying anybody, I mean."

Cameron said, "And you're sure it was a kidnap attempt,
not a hit."

"Right. We've found quite a bit of stuff that they dropped, presumably when Dane opened up." He tapped the
pad on the clipboard. "A pair of handcuffs, a roll of duct
tape, a hypodermic syringe—contents not yet analyzed,
of course, but it's safe to bet it's not insulin or Vita-
min B."

I said, "One of them yelled something about not shooting
at the house, they didn't want to hit Raintree. At least I
assumed it was Raintree they meant."

"Ah." Leonard made more notes. "Interesting. Bears out
the evidence. Speak Arabic, do you?"

Cameron guffawed. "Better than you speak English, son.
Also French, Spanish, Swahili, Vietnamese—"

"If it helps," I said, "the dialect was Syrian. Of course
they speak Syrian Arabic in Lebanon and some other areas,
too. But they definitely weren't Libyan."

Leonard was scribbling madly. "Yes, that *is* valuable
information . . . but nothing else you heard or saw gave
you any indication who they might be?"

"National origins, political affiliations, that sort of thing?
No."

"There's a million of these little terrorist outfits," Cameron said. "Or it seems like it anyway. They're like rock groups—a new one every day and you can't keep track of them all. And believe me, underneath the bullshit about the poor downtrodden Palestinians and the religious fanaticism, most of them are nothing in the world but Middle East versions of the Los Angeles street gangs. Bunch of young assholes with way to hell more firepower than brains, operating in a crazy environment where the rules have broken down and there's no one with the power or the will to do anything about them, so they run wild."

He was looking at Leonard, talking to him rather than me. Well, I had good reason to know these things already, and Cameron knew it.

"And like every other independent operation," he went on, "they have to have some kind of capital, something to support them in their chosen lifestyle. . . . In L.A. it's dope. In the Middle East it's politics and religion—line up with the Iranians or the Iraqis or the Libyans, and in exchange for a little bombing, a few assassinations, the odd hostage, why, you get a steady flow of cash and hardware. Dane knows what I'm talking about."

I said, "But that's all starting to fall apart, now the Iranians are nearly burned out and the Russians aren't bankrolling much of anybody any more."

"Exactly," Cameron said, nodding. "And so you've got Arafat and the boys trying to turn respectable, and other groups coming in for talks here and there, and down at the bottom of the dogpile, you've got these little jackoff outfits, the real crazies, starting to get a little desperate. They've blown any shot at turning straight and giving up the life, even if they had sense enough to do it; their only hope now is to pull off something really big, something to give them the capital to survive."

"You think that's what this was all about?" I asked Cameron. "One of the radical-fringe terrorist groups trying to make a big score?"

"Well, you've got to admit it would work. Considering the way the United States goes into massive paralysis over ordinary hostages nobody's ever heard of, the mind boggles at what they could do with a prisoner like Jerry Raintree."

"Whereas God knows what sort of retaliation might come down if they killed him," Leonard said thoughtfully. "Interesting theory. Well, we'll go over all this stuff and see if we can develop anything to point to their identity."

I said, "Just one thing before you haul everything away. I want one of those AK-47s."

Leonard frowned. "I'm afraid—"

"I'm afraid too. Out here on this island alone, I'm a hell of a lot afraider than you are. I won't be here much longer, and I don't really think they're going to come back, but you never know. Unless you've got something else I can have, leave the AK. And some ammo."

Cameron said, "It's okay, Leonard. I'll fix it. Leave him the piece. Christ knows you've earned it," he said to me. "Saved my pension, if nothing else."

"All right. I'll see to it," Leonard said. "Dane—*are* you going to be here if we need to ask more questions?"

"If I'm not," I said, "Cameron or somebody in the Company will know how to get hold of me."

Leonard nodded and started back down the steps. Cameron looked at me. "Figuring on going back to work, are you?"

"I think it's time. I was supposed to be recuperating, getting myself back together." I gestured at the scene below. "Looks like I've done that, wouldn't you say?"

"Well, yeah, now you put it that way. Hate to think of the carnage if you were in any *better* shape." He grinned and got out another cigarette. "Going back to Europe, or where?"

"I haven't decided."

"Well, do me a favor. If you're not in a big hurry, stick around here another couple of weeks, would you? I've got a man," he said, lighting up, "going to be coming out of the hospital, got himself busted up in a little jump accident, I figured he could take over on the island while he's mending. If you could see your way clear to staying till he's available?"

I shrugged. "I don't see why not. It's been getting a little boring—" I stopped, realizing what I'd just said, and we both broke up. "All right," I said after a minute, "but you know what I mean. A couple of weeks tops."

"Thanks. It shouldn't be longer than that. In return I'll send out some feelers," he said, "see if I can line you up one or two good jobs. Say in some country where the men can't shoot straight and the women got no morals at all." He looked thoughtful. "No, hell, if I hear of one like that I'll go for it myself."

We stood in silence for a couple of minutes, watching Leonard's crew finishing up. One man was picking up empty brass and dropping the cases carefully into a little plastic bag. I couldn't figure out why. If you've seen one ejected 7.62mm. empty you've seen them all. Of course you could have said much the same thing about the two thugs in the body bags.

"I wish to Christ I could go *somewhere* for the next couple of weeks," Cameron said. "The paper work on this shit, you can imagine. And that's not to mention the *real* swamp full of alligators waiting for me to wade."

He turned and gave me a look that had absolutely no humor in it. "Because, you know," he said, "we haven't said a word yet about the big question, have we?"

I suppose I looked blank. He said impatiently, "Oh, come on, Dane, don't tell me it hasn't even occurred to you yet."

It hit me then. Well, I'd had a tiring and sleepless night; even so, I felt thick as the redwood planks we were standing on. I said, "Son of a bitch."

Cameron was nodding, his face taut and grim. "Yes indeed. Son of a bitch. Very much son of a bitch. Question is, which son of a bitch?"

He waved his hand in a gesture that included the house and the island and the men swarming over it. "All this complicated routine we ran, here and Houston and D.C., making sure nobody knew where Raintree was—even ordinary people who might call the news people—and believe me, Dane, it got real fancy up at the other end, with all those nosy Washington journalists to worry about. And then those ragheads show up, and it's clear that they knew exactly where he was and when he was going to be there—"

"Considering how long it's been since Billy Jumper first saw that plane," I said, "they had their information well in advance."

"Damn straight. In fact they must have known just about as soon as I did. Which brings us to the big one: *how the hell did they know?*" He threw his cigarette over the railing with an angry gesture. "We got a leak somewhere, Dane. Going to be hell to pay, running it down."

I said, "Maybe the leak's in Raintree's office, not the Company."

"That's not good news either, if that's where it is. Raintree's on the House Intelligence Committee, remember? All sorts of sensitive stuff could get leaked there."

A man came out of the house holding a metal toolbox in one hand and some electronic circuitry in the other. "Can't fix it here," he said to Cameron. "Got to take it back to

Houston, try to get some replacement parts. You want the details?"

"Hell, no, I wouldn't understand a word. Just do it." Cameron looked at me as the man clumped down the steps. "Tech wienies. God save us from them."

"So now I've got no outside communications at all. Great," I said. "I hope Ali and his buddies aren't planning a return visit."

"Hell, why would they?" Cameron said. "Just to get even for the two punks you whacked? After all, they were legitimate fire-fight casualties; it's not like you murdered them. Like, uh." He stopped, his face turning red. "Sorry."

"Like Abdelkader? Sure. But it wouldn't make any difference, by Arab rules. Revenge is a sacred duty in that part of the world, and it doesn't matter whether the guy you were avenging had it coming. Hell, they've got blood feuds in the Middle East that go back over a thousand years."

"Sure, but that's on their home grounds. Coming back here to get even, when their original mission is blown and they know we're looking for them—I can't see it," Cameron said. "My money says they're not even in the country any more. With that seaplane they could be anywhere along the Mexican coast or one of the Caribbean islands. If it's amphibious, which it could be since we don't know the make, the possibilities go right off the screen."

"Cuba?" I suggested.

"Could be. Could very damn well be. Fidel still has some ties with some of those groups, and he's running on a pretty lean mixture himself lately. They must have had *some* kind of outside help, somewhere to stage from and refuel on their way back home."

"I hope you're right," I said. "But just in case you're not, I'm still hanging onto that AK-47." I jerked my thumb at the nearby doorway. "And I'm moving into the house for the rest of my time here. Up here, I can look in all directions and see trouble coming a hell of a lot better than I can in that damn tin can of a trailer. Any problem with that?"

Cameron shrugged. "No problem at all. Time my report goes in, you're going to be one popular fellow in the Company. Nobody's going to mind if you cut yourself a few extra perks."

I said, "Who do I have to shoot to qualify for some peace and quiet?"

"You find out," Cameron said, "tell me about it, I'll shoot the son of a bitch myself."

By the time everybody finally left, the sun was going down and I was starting to lurch a little. No sleep last night, and not all that much the two nights before, thanks to Brenda. Well, and thanks to myself as well; I hadn't after all, fought her off with a club. I made an effort to stop thinking of Brenda.

Standing inside the trailer, wondering if I should move into the house tonight or wait till tomorrow, I heard an outboard approaching. It wasn't as big as the Zodiac motors and I thought I recognized it, but I picked up the AK-47 anyway before going to see.

It was Billy Jumper, holding a string of fish. "Thought you might be hungry," he said. "All that excitement last night."

I took the fish and he said, "You going to be all right, Dane? I mean really."

"If I can get some sleep."

"Sure. You look beat, son." He hesitated. "Look, do you want me to come out here and sort of stand watch while you catch up on your rest? In case the A-rabs come back?"

I said, "Thanks, but it's not necessary. They won't be coming back."

"Sure of that, are you?"

I sighed. "Why not? That's the considered and expert opinion of a senior officer of the organization that predicted that the Cubans would rise and support the Bay of Pigs invasion, that the Viet Cong couldn't possibly mount a serious offensive, and that the Iraqis would never dare attack Kuwait. I mean, Billy, how can you question authority like that?"

He took off his hat and scratched his head. "Say what?" he said. "You want to run that horse by me again, I didn't get too good a look at him first time out of the stall."

"Never mind." I remembered something. "Did you get your boat back?"

"Oh, sure. That fellow Cameron brought it over. They had me looking at some pictures in a book, seeing if I could spot what kind of plane it was I saw. Think I picked the right one but who knows? Comes to airplanes, I know a lot about boats."

"Well, thanks for the use of it last night. And thanks for showing up in that cop boat when you did," I said. "You probably kept us all from being killed."

He looked slightly embarrassed. "You think it worked? I felt like a damn fool."

"Believe me, it worked. Thanks again." I hoisted the fish in one hand. "And for these too."

I watched him motor back toward the mainland, a small dark shape against a bay turned the color of blood.

Back at the trailer, I took a couple of the smaller fish off the stringer and put them out for Raoul. Then I put the rest in the freezer—it had been a nice thought, but there was no way in hell I was up to cleaning and frying a lot of fish right now—and stood for a moment considering the alternatives.

Finally I went up to the house and had a look in the kitchen. As I'd hoped, the refrigerator still held several of Brenda's frozen dinners. I stuck one into the microwave and checked the electric coffee pot. Still half full; been sitting there since last night and nobody remembering to turn it off. It was going to taste like crankcase drippings but I didn't care; my taste buds had gone to sleep anyway. I poured myself a cup of sludge and laid the AK-47 across the table and sat down while the microwave did its mysterious business.

The coffee was even worse than I'd expected; I wondered which of them had made it. Glancing around, I saw that the place was in something of a mess, the sink full of dirty dishes, the table littered with glasses and cups. Well, they'd had to leave in something of a hurry. I'd straighten up tomorrow.

Done with dinner, I threw the cardboard tray into the overflowing wastebasket—going to have to make a garbage run over to Bayport tomorrow too; I should have gotten Leonard to take the trash along for analysis—and picked up the AK-47 and walked wearily into the bedroom.

The bed was in a mess too. That was no surprise, under the circumstances. It was messy in a way that suggested perhaps Ali and his friends had picked a particularly awkward time to come around. A single black sock lay in the middle of the floor; no doubt Jerry and Brenda had packed in considerable haste. I looked at the bed a minute and decided I wasn't quite tired enough to sleep on the same sheets they'd been screwing on.

I stripped the sheets off the bed, balled them up, and stuffed them into the laundry hamper in the little hallway. After a brief search I located fresh sheets on a shelf in the closet. When I bent down to make the bed I saw something sticking out from underneath.

More clothing; maybe I ought to hold a garage sale. I reached down and picked the object up and found I was holding a black nylon garter belt.

It was much too big for Brenda. It could only have been worn by someone about the size of, oh. . . .

I picked up the AK-47 and headed for the door. Somehow I'd just decided to sleep in the trailer tonight after all.

10

•••••

FRIDAY I MOVED INTO THE HOUSE ANYWAY; AS I'd told Cameron, I felt the need of a better view of anything that might be coming my way. Whatever weird scenes might have taken place in the bedroom, it wasn't worth throwing away a tactical advantage just to indulge my personal aversions.

I cleaned up the place, more or less, and washed the dishes. A stray round had shattered one of the windows, and I had a hell of a job getting all the broken glass up. I hauled one of the plywood sheets up from under the house and nailed it over the broken window; probably I was supposed to board the other windows back up too, but I wasn't about to blind myself.

For some reason I had it in my head that Brenda might have left me some sort of note, but I didn't find anything. Well, she'd been a little preoccupied at the time. She hadn't even spoken to me that night; I'd only seen her once, on her way out to the helicopter, and she hadn't looked my way.

Raoul came around while I was carrying out the trash. It was the first time I'd seen him since Wednesday, though the food I'd put out for him had vanished during the night. Even now, he was being careful; he made a thorough and efficient search of the house, checking all the blind spots and sniffing at the closet doors, before he was satisfied. Smart cat, I thought as I got him a can of tuna fish, he knew something a lot of people never learned—don't be too quick to assume it's over just because the guns have quit going off.

I loaded the sacks of trash in the skiff and motored over to Bayport, where I gave Billy Jumper a few bucks to truck it up to Soto to the landfill. Heading back across the bay, the sea wind in my face and the bright sun sparkling off the wavetops, I felt myself begin to relax a little, the tightness inside me starting to slack. Hell, I'd been around the block too many times to let myself go paranoid like this; I was getting as jumpy as the damn cat.

All the same, when I got back to the island, I took the AK-47 down to the point and fired a few rounds at bits of driftwood, then a couple of full-auto bursts, just to make sure it was working all right. I got the shotgun and reloaded it, too; and after a brief hesitation I found the Dragoon pistol where I'd tossed it Wednesday night, took it apart and cleaned it, and reloaded it. It had done the job for me once, and if I was going to have it around it might as well be ready for use.

That night I sat on the couch in the living room, drinking Lone Star and listening to the radio. They played a record I hadn't heard in years, an old Porter Wagoner classic about a man who comes home a day early from an out-of-town trip and decides to show up with a bottle of champagne to surprise his wife. At the liquor store he hears a stranger bragging about the married woman he's on his way to see, but it doesn't register because the man doesn't know the cold hard facts of life.

As he leaves the liquor store he notices the stranger driving along right in front of him; he finds himself on the stranger's tail all the way to his own house, where the stranger turns into his driveway. At last he knows the cold hard facts of life.

So he drives around and around the block, drinking the champagne and listening to the sounds coming from his house, and finally he stops the car and gets out and goes into the house and kills both of them. And, he says, now he's going to spend the rest of his life in a cell, but he sure taught them the cold hard facts of life. . . .

I went and got a pillow and a blanket and bedded down on the couch. I'd rigged up a few little surprises, around the house and on the steps and the deck, in case anyone came around; but no one did.

The weather stayed clear and warm. Gradually the feeling of menace began to go away; life returned to something like its normal routine. I resumed my runs along the beach—carrying the AK-47, now, but even that was mostly to help build up my arms and shoulders—and by Sunday afternoon I felt safe enough to go for a long swim. By then I'd even quit grabbing the rifle and diving for cover every time a stray motorboat wandered too close to the island.

Monday I still hadn't gotten my radiotelephone back. I took the skiff over to Bayport and called Cameron from the pay phone outside the store.

"For God's sake, Cameron," I said when I finally reached him. "How long does it take to fix a simple damn ship-to-shore? Or just replace it, for that matter?"

"I've got them on it," he said. "Probably be a couple more days tops. Problem is it's not one of our standard sets. It's some off-the-wall outfit the dopers were using, our people don't have parts for it. But if we replace it there's channels to go through, might take longer. I'm doing all I can."

He sounded strange; there was a funny strained note in his voice. I said, "Is something the matter? Anything I need to know about?"

There was a pause, so long I was starting to wonder if we'd lost the connection. But then there came a long sigh and Cameron said slowly, "I'm not sure, Dane. Some straws in the wind, you might say. Nothing I can nail down just yet . . . anyway, it's not something I can talk about over a public telephone."

"Anything yet on who those guys were?"

"Like I said, Dane, we can't talk about it on the phone. Look, I'll come down there," he said, "soon as I know anything, we can talk then. Maybe I'll have a new RT for you by then."

I said thanks and started to hang up. "Dane?" he said, still in that strained voice. "Be careful, will you?"

I put the phone back on its hook and made a face at my own reflection in the store window. What the hell was going on? Just when my paranoia was beginning to let up, Cameron had to start acting mysterious.

I started to walk back toward the dock. A voice said, "Hi there!"

I swung around and saw a tall, skinny kid sitting behind the wheel of a parked Jeep. He had screaming red hair and a sunburn. I recognized him now; he'd been one of the gang I'd run off the island, one of Ray's buddies.

"Hey, no sweat," he said quickly, holding up his hands, palms outward. "Look, I'm sorry as hell about that trouble we had. We's just drunk, you know? That ol' Ray, he's about half mean he gets a few in him. He ast for what you give him."

He laughed, a braying loose-lipped guffaw that would have peeled paint off a tank. "Ol' Ray's in jail now," he said. "Driving drunk, he got into a chase with a bunch of highway cops up by Galveston, run off the road and wrecked his car and then started fighting with them when they come up. You work for the govment, don't you?" he said suddenly.

"My cousin Jim Bob, he's a depitty up at Soto, he says that island's some kind of secret govment place, everybody's supposed to stay clear. Damn, we wouldn't of gone near if we'd of known. You oughta put signs up."

I said with a straight face, "It wouldn't be secret then, would it?"

He considered this. "I guess not. I heard all that shooting out there the other night. Me and my girl was parked down by the bay, you know? People shooting off machine guns out there, boy, I guess we're lucky you didn't just mow us all down."

He shook his head. "I'm real sorry we bothered you," he repeated earnestly.

I said, "It's all right."

Actually, it occurred to me that I owed him and the other idiots a strange kind of debt. If it hadn't been for them—even Ray; especially Ray—I wouldn't have bought the .44, and Wednesday night's affair would have found me unarmed.

"I'm going in the Army next month myself," he said proudly as I started to walk away. "I wanta be one of them Green Berets."

I shook my head, brushing away the mental pictures. "Good luck," I said sincerely.

Down at the boat dock Billy Jumper said, "Saw you talking to Red up by the store. He give you any trouble?"

"No." I climbed down into the skiff. "Just telling me about his upcoming military career."

"Should of told him to put in for West Point," Billy said drily, tossing me the line. "That boy's officer material if I ever saw it. Hell, they'll probably make him a general."

Tuesday was when I finally got hit in the face by the cold hard facts of life.

There was no warning and no foreboding. It was another bright hot day, the sky almost painfully blue. Even the sea birds' constant squawking had a cheerful sound. Loping around the island that morning, I told myself that I was going to miss this place and this life; if I had any sense, I thought, I'd raise the money somehow and buy myself an island like this and get out of the business for good.

After my swim I went up to the house for a beer and discovered that the supply of Lone Star was getting dangerously low. A little looking around turned up a number of other shortages in less vital but still important areas, such as food, and a check of the trailer failed to fill the shortages. One more grocery run, then; I'd been hoping to be out of here before anything else ran out.

I took the skiff over to Bayport and tied up at Billy Jumper's dock, leaving the AK-47 hidden under an old tarp in the bow—I didn't like leaving it at all, but the tolerance of the local law might not extend quite that far—and went and found the old man. He wasn't hard to find; even before I got out of the boat I could hear his voice coming from the shed:

> *"Um anijus um anijus*
> *Emekusupkun um anijus—"*

He got up as I entered the shed, wiping his hands on his ragged jeans. An outboard motor lay partly disassembled on the floor. I said, "What was that you were singing?"

"Old Seminole Baptist hymn. Means—" He screwed his face up in thought. " 'Help me to pray,' that's what it means."

"Want to be a taxi driver again for awhile?"

"Why not?" He kicked at the stripped-down motor with a bare foot. "Got to pay better than the boat business. Let me get my shoes."

But the old pickup developed a flat halfway back from Soto, and we had a sweaty time changing it. By the time I got back and pointed the skiff toward the island, it was getting late, the sun starting to touch the flat horizon of the coastal plain.

I made a slow circuit of the island before heading in, checking the beach for signs of visitors. I didn't really take the danger seriously any more, but it was a habit I wasn't quite ready to break. I saw nothing out of the ordinary, no boats, no tracks except my own. A little irritably, I turned the skiff in to the dock and tied up.

I set the grocery sacks and the case of beer up onto the dock, slung the AK-47 over my shoulder, and hoisted myself up. It was going to take two trips to get it all up to the house; starting up the board walkway, the beer under one arm and the Kalashnikov under the other, I suddenly realized that I hadn't eaten since lunch. Have to take care of that; say the little steaks I'd bought in Soto, give Raoul the bones to play with. . . .

The sun was behind the live-oaks now, the long shadows falling across the area around the house. I had my foot on the bottom step before I saw what they'd done.

Raoul wouldn't be eating the leftovers tonight, or any other night. They'd disemboweled him, then spread his paws and nailed him to one of the pilings in a horrible parody of crucifixion. His head had been smashed in; I hoped they'd done that first. Somehow he looked smaller, just a bloody swatch of fur hanging there in the shadows.

My stomach convulsed violently, but I fought down the need to vomit; this was no time to lose control. I dropped flat, letting the beer fall to the sand, bringing the AK-47 up and ready, scanning the area rapidly but carefully, while the hair stood up on my neck. Even with the pilings for cover, I was dead if they were still there and wanted to pick me off.

After a long, stomach-churning wait, I eased myself up onto my knees, ready to drop again at any sound or movement; and finally, with all my nerve-ends howling a protest, I stood up, flattening myself against a piling. Still there was nothing.

Moving slowly, keeping close to whatever cover was available, I studied the area. There were tracks here and there, quite a few of them. They'd been at the trailer, where they'd forced the door open but hadn't bothered anything inside, and they'd checked the concrete blockhouse but didn't seem to have gone in. There were no tracks going toward the beach or coming from it; they must have come in over the dock and up the walkway.

I couldn't tell whether they'd gone inland. There were no tracks going back from the living area into the dunes, but tracks could have been brushed away; the sea-oats made it hard to read sign. And the wind would have covered any tracks, anyway, if they'd been there very long.

I considered walking along the beach, checking for sign, or even working my way through the grasses and the dunes, searching the interior of the island. But there was no sense in that; if they were still on the island, they could ambush me anywhere. Right here, I had the best defensive position, the most cover and the best view. If they were still here and they wanted me, they could come get me; I wasn't going to make it that easy for them.

There still remained the house. I'd been putting that off; the possibilities were just too scary. If they were sitting up there right now, laughing up their sleeves, just waiting for me to come up the steps so they could blow my head off. . . .

Cursing myself for a damn fool, knowing I should have already gotten the hell off the island, I climbed slowly up the redwood steps. My gut felt very tight as I raised my head above the level of the deck; my pupils were probably the size of manhole covers. But still nobody killed me. I dived through the door, gun at the ready, and then did a nerve-stretching search of the rooms. Except for nearly shooting myself in the bedroom mirror, nothing happened.

The house was an anti-climax, in fact; they hadn't even vandalized the place. They'd gone through things pretty sloppily, dumping clothes on the floor and leaving the refrigerator open, but the impression was one of idle curiosity rather than a systematic search.

They hadn't entirely wasted their time, though. The gun cabinet was open and the shotgun was gone. The .44 was also gone from the bedside table.

I went back out on the deck, keeping low, and had a slow careful look-around with the binoculars I'd found in the trailer. Nothing.

So they were either still on the island or not, and no way of telling except by going out asking to get killed. There was really only one thing to do now; much as I'd have liked to shoot a few of the bastards, the situation was clearly impossible. They had the numbers and the firepower and the organization. What I had was a boat and a clear run for it; it was time to take it.

I went back down the ladder fast, hitting the ground running, wondering if they were going to let me go; it might have all been their idea of a joke, letting me screw around here and then blowing me away as I ran for the boat . . . but when I got down to the dock I saw that they'd thought of something better.

The skiff was gone.

I pulled up the mooring line and looked at the dangling end. Cut with a hell of a sharp knife; I threw it down in disgust and looked out across the bay. Sure enough, I could see the skiff drifting slowly on the sunset-tinged waves, being carried inexorably out to sea by the outgoing tide. If I hadn't been so intent on scanning the island for bad guys, I'd have seen it from the cabin.

For one crazy moment I thought about swimming after it. But it was too far—maybe not for a Navy SEAL, maybe not even for me when I was fifteen years younger, but too far for me now. And if I didn't make it, I'd never get back to land against the tide.

I walked slowly back up to the house, no longer bothering to be careful. Obviously they weren't planning to kill me just yet—or if they were, there wasn't much I could do about it; if one of them didn't get me another one would. I got the hammer from the storeroom and pulled the nails out and took Raoul down and went back to the storeroom for a shovel. The hell with them; there was something I was going to do.

I buried what was left of Raoul up under the live-oaks, digging deep so the sand wouldn't blow away and uncover him. Poor bastard, he was a casualty of my failure to remember the cold hard facts of life. . . .

I went back up to the house and poured myself a Wild Turkey and sat on the couch for a moment, thinking. There was no way to get a distress call out to Cameron or anyone else, thanks to that damn RT; and the authorities on the mainland—and, thanks to at least one bigmouthed deputy, the civilians as well—had been well and truly taught to take no note of gunfire or other sounds from the island. I should have bought a flare pistol and told Billy Jumper to watch out for signals, but it was too late to think of that now. Possibly if I set the cabin on fire? It might work, but—

I tossed back the rest of the drink and slammed the glass down on the coffee table and stood up. The hell with it; I was tired of the game, tired of being played with. Let them come and do whatever they were here to do, if they could; I'd damn well see to it they had an interesting time of it. If I was on my own, well, that was how I liked it. At least I wouldn't have to worry about hitting friendlies.

Besides, the sons of bitches had killed my cat.

I waited until the light was fading and then I went back down and spent some time arranging various traps and warning devices. Most of my efforts were pretty crude, and there was no way to do anything really nasty; the sand was too loose for a pit trap and there was no vegetation suitable for constructing the ever-popular Malayan Gate and its variations. But at least I might give myself a little advance warning if my guests came calling in the night— even though I was certain they were watching me the whole time, probably making notes. You do what you can. . . .

Then I went back up to the house and stuck a frozen dinner into the microwave. I didn't feel like eating, but I was going to need my strength. While the food cooked, I made up a pot of strong coffee. It was going to be a very long night, or else a very short one; but either way, I planned to be awake and ready for whatever came.

It *was* a long night. Not the longest I'd ever spent, by any means—long nights, after all, are something of an occupational hazard in my line—but long enough.

Not that things got all that rugged. On the contrary, it was simply boring. Nothing happened. No guns went off, nobody set fire to the house or lobbed explosives through the windows; the lights continued to burn, even though a six-year-old kid could have gotten into that power room and shut down the generator or just yanked the main switch on the breaker box. The only sounds from outside were the wind and the surf down on the beach. They didn't even call out insults or demands for surrender.

Along about midnight I went so far as to construct a fairly realistic dummy from some clothes and blankets and stand it at an open window, thinking perhaps they'd take a shot at it. They didn't; all I got for my efforts was a feeling that there was a second dummy in the house. I tried flicking the floodlights off and on at irregular intervals, hoping to catch somebody moving around, but all that did was confuse the mosquitoes.

More than once I played with the idea that perhaps they weren't there at all; perhaps they'd already left. There was no logical reason for them to go away, but then there had been no logical reason that I could see for them to be here in the first place. The waves and the wind would have covered the sound of throttled-back motors. It was possible I was going through all this nonsense for no reason at all; I might be playing this comedy to an empty house.

But I didn't believe it for a minute. They were out there. Corny as it might sound, I could feel them.

And it was obvious by now that they had very specific plans and weren't going to be tempted into deviating from them. They didn't want to kill me here and now; they'd had too many chances to do that. All too clearly, they were trying to take me alive.

Which was a far from comforting thought. You don't have to have my years of Middle East experience to know that being captured by their kind is an ugly prospect; most nights, the six o'clock news will do just fine.

I wondered, though, what they thought they were going to accomplish by snatching me. Surely they didn't think I was hostage material, a replacement for Raintree. Nobody in the world was going to give them anything for Randall Dane. I doubted if they'd even be able to find anyone willing to admit I existed.

The single-digit hours crawled by. It was like pulling interior guard all over again, with no relief on the way and no Sergeant of the Guard to call in any case not covered by instructions. I drank a lot of black coffee and pissed a great deal. Maybe that was what they were up to, getting me to kill myself with kidney failure. The night's battle was turning out to be a battle to stay awake.

Maybe, I thought, that was their game; maybe they were simply wearing me down, taking the edge off my responses against the hour when they finally made their move. If that was the idea, it was working. And there wasn't a damn thing I could do about it.

The sky was just starting to yellow out to sea, the bad light of false dawn filtering through the windows, when I heard the sound of a motor coming up the inshore channel toward the island. It was moving fast, making plenty of racket, and I had no trouble at all recognizing it. I'd been listening for that distinctive note for a week now.

I got a brief look through the glasses as the Zodiac bounced toward me, swinging out to clear the shoal water off the point. One man sat in the stern, a dark, bearded figure in a camo T-shirt; his left arm, I saw with interest, appeared to be heavily bandaged and supported by a sling.

There was a moment when I could have picked him off from the window; the range was reasonable and he wasn't moving all that fast, and it would have cut the odds down a little. I laid the Kalashnikov's sights on him and thought about it and decided against it. Almost certainly, I'd hole that inflatable boat in the process, and then his buddies would be trapped on the island with me—and while I didn't think I had much chance of running them off, I didn't like to close off the possibility. And there just might be a chance, later on, for me to get my hands on that boat.

Anyway, I only had the one thirty-round magazine— they'd gotten all my ammo supply but what was in the gun, yesterday—and I didn't figure I should use up cartridges on a man who was already wounded.

The Zodiac disappeared around the point; I heard its engine shutting down as it approached the dock. A neat little bit of business that had been, sending the boat away so I'd walk unsuspecting into the trap; I wondered where the other Zodiac was. I hoped it wasn't on the way with reinforcements.

It was getting lighter outside. Time to reconsider my situation. The house had made a good defensive position at night; by day it left a lot to be desired. Sooner or later they were going to smoke me out; the walls weren't thick enough to stop a 7.62mm. bullet—I'd checked that out by personal experiment last week—and there was no really solid furniture to use for barricades. And then they might have CS gas—

There was a sudden sharp coughing bang somewhere outside. A window shattered and I turned just as a flare burst into blinding flame in the middle of the living room floor. The carpet began to curl back and burn. Thick smoke billowed up and filled the room, lit weirdly by the dazzling white light of the flare.

Coughing, I ran for the kitchen and grabbed the red chemical fire extinguisher that hung above the counter, snapping the safety band free and flipping the lever up as I charged back into the living room. The flare was already burning its way into the floor; the boards were catching fire all around it. I triggered the fire extinguisher, hoping the damn thing was fully charged. There was a loud farting sound and whitish clouds of some sort of dry chemical burst from the nozzle, blanketing the fire.

The flames around the flare began to die down almost instantly. The flare itself seemed barely affected; I remembered that it was nearly impossible to extinguish a marine flare. But if I could keep the floor from catching fire, I figured the flare would burn clear through in a few minutes and drop harmlessly to the sand below.

Another flare landed on the sun deck outside. A moment later a bedroom window broke.

So much for playing fireman; this had gotten impossible. I grabbed the AK-47 and kicked open the door and rushed out onto the deck, jumping over the burning flare, moving at a run toward the steps and keeping low in a crouch. I wondered if they'd nail me at the bottom or wait and surround me somewhere back in the dunes. Maybe I ought to jump over the rail; it was only ten feet or so and soft sand at the bottom. But there was no one in sight around the foot of the stairway, and I headed down, taking the steps two at a time.

If I'd been a little more alert, if my eyes hadn't been stinging from the smoke, I might have seen it in time. I felt the taut wire dig into my shins for a fraction of a second; then I was airborne, flying gracelessly out away from the steps, seeing the sand coming up at me too fast even to tuck and roll. I slammed down hard on my chest, the wind going out of me in a sickening *unh!* while the AK-47 went flying.

Before I could even raise my face out of the sand, a body landed heavily on top of me, then another, pinning me down. I felt the round hard coldness of a rifle muzzle against the back of my neck.

A voice said, "No move. No move."

I kept very still. Somewhere nearby another voice was shouting in Arabic; it sounded like Ali. "Up there and put out those fires!" he yelled. "If the house burns, someone might see the smoke and come from the mainland." There was a muffled reply and Ali said impatiently, "Carry some sand and pour on the flares, of course. Just like a fire bomb, you know."

Someone called, "I saw a fire extinguisher in the trailer yesterday."

"Then get it, in the name of God, and use it, before the house is ablaze." There was a pause and then Ali's voice came from much nearer. "You have him? Is he unhurt?"

"I think so."

"Good. By God, that is good." There was a soft slapping sound that might have been Ali clapping his hands together. "Secure him. You know what to do."

Someone grabbed my wrists and yanked my arms around behind my back. I felt handcuffs snap into place, very tight, the metal biting into my wrists.

"Now," Ali said, "let him up, but watch him and be ready . . . on your feet," he said in English. "No tricks, okay?"

He'd wasted that last warning, I thought sourly as I struggled to my feet. I was clear out of the trick business this morning. I didn't seem to be much good at it.

"Dane," Ali said, beaming, as I faced him. "You've made us work very hard. So glad I am finally getting to meet you again."

11

•••••

HE STOOD THERE GIVING ME HIS BIG SMILE, enjoying himself. Well, he had some right; he'd played his hand perfectly this time. He was still wearing nothing but skin and muscles and curly black hair from the waist up, but he'd changed the shorts for desert-camo fatigue pants. A holstered pistol, some sort of heavy automatic, hung from a military web belt. In one hand he held an AK-47, the muzzle not quite pointed at me.

He said, "Stand completely still, Dane," and to one of the goons holding me, in Arabic, "Search him."

I stood there and let the bastard paw me up and down; he didn't do a very good job but it didn't matter because I didn't have anything on me that would do me any good or him any harm. He found the ring of keys in my pocket and tossed them to Ali. "Nothing else," he said.

A man came up, holding out a rifle, looking pissed off. He was a skinny, wild-looking character, even darker than the others; I didn't think he'd been with Ali that day they'd come to check the island out.

"Look," he said to Ali. "He was carrying Hussein's rifle. I recognize it by that crack in the handgrip." To me, still in Arabic, he said, "American pig, you killed my brother," and swung back the Kalashnikov for a buttstroke. I pulled back against the men holding me, but Ali raised a hand and stopped the blow.

"Not now, Zaal," he said almost gently. "When the time comes, he will pay for everything. By my God, he will pay."

His eyes were on my face rather than Zaal's. I kept my expression blank as he added, "You understand what I am saying, don't you, you son of a diseased whore? Answer or I will let Zaal kill you slowly."

He paused, studying me. "No?" he said in English. "I was thinking maybe you speak Arabic. Well, perhaps not." To the others he said in Arabic, "He may know our language and he may not. Be careful what you say in front of him."

Zaal seemed to want to continue the confrontation, but Ali took the AK-47 from him and gave him a light shove. "Go on, now. Help the others put out the fires."

I said, "Nice little trick with the flares. But why did you wait so long? Afraid I might get away in the dark?"

He laughed. "Ah, but we were waiting for Ishak to come back with the boat. The flare gun was in the boat, you see."

"What happened to your other boat?"

"Oh, your waters around here are very tricky, Dane." He shook his head. "Very—what is it? Not deep—shallow, yes, very shallow in places. We struck something in the dark and broke the propeller."

That was the third time he'd called me by my name. I wanted very badly to ask him some questions about that, but I knew I wouldn't get any answers.

I said, "Okay, it was a pretty damn professional little job. You got me and you didn't lose any more men doing it." His grin got even broader and I went on, "The only thing I don't understand—when you did everything else so slick, why that sicko business with the cat? Christ, the Mau Mau wore that old gag out back in the Fifties. Did you think it would scare me? All it did was warn me you were here."

He was nodding, the grin gone. "You are absolutely right, you know. It was a stupid thing. Zaal and a couple of the others did it while I was down on the beach with the boat. The motor was running and I did not hear until too late." He scowled. "Believe me, I gave them the devil for that. You might have gotten away."

Behind him, a big husky fellow in camo fatigues came down the ladder, his face smudged with smoke. "The fire is out," he said to Ali. "The house is still full of smoke."

"Good." Ali threw an arm around his shoulders. "This is Ahmad," he said to me. "He was the one who swam to your boat and set it adrift."

Ahmad favored me with a baleful stare. This wasn't a no-hard-feelings, all-in-the-game affair; these bastards clearly hated me with all their tiny twisted souls. I wondered what the story was. I was pretty certain I was going to find out soon.

The rest of the Scabby Bunch were gathering around now. I counted seven, including Ali; then the skinny one with the bandaged arm came up the walkway from the dock and made it eight. I noticed that he was carrying a submachine gun rather than one of the ever-popular AK-47s; a much less effective weapon at any range, it would still be handier for a man with one arm in a sling.

Ali said, "Ah, Ishak! I'm afraid you must go back again. I have to send a message to Jesus."

He pronounced it *Hay-zoos*, Spanish style; in Arabic it would have been "Isa." If Jesus was the pilot of the sea-plane, as I guessed, the implications were fascinating.

Ishak looked annoyed. As walking wounded, he was getting stuck with all the errand-boy jobs. But he didn't protest. He said, "What do you want me to tell him?"

"Have him bring the airplane up this evening," Ali said, "as soon as it is dark, and not before, you understand? I don't want to take any more risks when there is no need. These waters are full of boats, but the airplane will surely be noticed. And the Americans take great interest in strange airplanes along this coast, because of drug smugglers. Tell him to wait until dark and fly low."

Ahmad said, "Ali, you know that Jesus does not like to land on the water at night. He says it is difficult and dangerous."

Ali spat on the sand. "Jesus is not employed to fly the airplane when he wants to do so. He is paid to fly when *we* wish it. And that Cuban dog knows nothing at all of difficulty, let alone risk." To Ishak he said, "He may come just before sunset, if he must, but no sooner. You will stay and come with him. Make sure he follows orders."

Ishak grinned nastily and lifted the Ingram. "He will do as you wish."

"In God's name, don't kill him," Ali said seriously. "Or we will never get home."

As Ishak disappeared down the walkway toward the dock, Ali turned back to me. "If you did not understand," he said in English, "and I still am not sure about that, we are going to be waiting now. When have you last eaten?"

"Last night," I said, puzzled. "Just after sunset."

"Good. Then it will not hurt to go a day without food. I do not want to make your hands free," he said, "until we are off this island, and I will not shame any of these men by making him feed you like a child. When we are on our way this evening, we will give you something to eat. Perhaps. If you make no trouble."

In Arabic he said, "I don't want to have to watch him all day. And if anyone should come, he might call out a warning or make noise. Take him out to that concrete building and lock him in the storeroom. Who has the tape—Gamal? Leave the handcuffs on and tape his ankles."

One of the men holding me—I recognized him by his scraggly beard; he had been in the Zodiac with Ali on their first visit—said, "Shall we gag him as well?"

"No reason for that, Gamal. It's always possible for a prisoner to choke to death if you gag him and don't watch him—you remember that Jew last year? Those concrete walls are very thick," Ali said, "and the door shuts tightly, and moreover there is a diesel engine in the next room. Let him shout until his throat is sore, if he likes. No one will hear him."

Ahmad said, "I don't like leaving him unwatched for so long, Ali. He might be able to get out of the handcuffs."

One of the others made a jeering sound. Ahmad said defensively, "Some of these American agents are trained to pick locks."

"Behind his back? But if he does get the handcuffs off, what then? He will still be locked inside the storeroom," Ali pointed out, "with no way to get at that big padlock outside. And there are no windows, not even a ventilator."

"He might attack the man who comes for him," Ahmad suggested.

Ali laughed. "A single unarmed man does not so easily overpower alert armed guards, my brother. You have seen too many films. And," he said as Ahmad started to object again, "at the worst, just to indulge your worries for a moment, what if he should somehow manage to get loose? This is a tiny island, it is daylight, there are seven of us with automatic rifles, and now Ishak has gone there will be no way off for anyone until Jesus comes with the airplane."

"We can look in on him from time to time," Gamal put in, "if Ahmad is so afraid of him."

Ali waved his hands to silence the angry response. "None of that, none of that. Ahmad, your concern for security is to be commended. We all understand that you are merely being careful." He gave Gamal a pointed look. "All of us have waited and prayed for a long time for this day. None of us wants him to escape now. But trust me, he will not do so."

To me, in English, he said, "Which of these keys opens the storeroom?"

I gave him a blank stare. He sighed. "Shall I have Zaal ask you, then?"

I said, "The big silver one."

Ali nodded and tossed the ring of keys to Gamal. "You have your instructions. I am going to the trailer to try and get some rest." He stretched, rather theatrically. "When he is secure, you may all take turns sleeping, if you like. I want two men up on that deck at all times, watching all approaches, but don't let yourselves be seen. Wake me if anyone seems to be coming toward the island to land. And someone should look in on the prisoner now and then, just in case Ahmad is right."

He gestured impatiently. "Go on, get him out of here. I am tired of looking at him."

They dragged me out to the blockhouse and threw me into the storeroom, knocking me to the floor with their rifle butts. Gamal did a sloppy-looking but highly effective job of taping my ankles together with silver duct tape; when he was done I could barely wiggle my toes. After looking me over a moment, he wrapped more tape around my wrists, over the handcuffs. "Now pick your way free, dog," he said as he stood up, and gave me a kick in the ribs.

The other one said, "Shall I leave the light on, Gamal? Ali said to check on him from time to time, and the light will make it easier."

Gamal stood for a moment scratching his ratty beard, considering the question. "Turn it off," he said finally. "Ahmad is an old woman, and Ali is getting almost as bad. Anyway, I for one would like to see this Ferengi bastard try to escape, so I might have the privilege of shooting him in the guts and watching him die. If it were up to me, we would have killed him already."

He spat in my direction. "Leave him on his belly in the darkness, like the unclean thing he is."

The light snapped off. A moment later the door thudded shut and I was alone in the dark.

For awhile—God knows how long; the darkness and the silence and the immobility destroyed all sense of time—I lay there, stretched out on the concrete floor, reviewing my options. They seemed pretty limited for now.

One good effort established that the duct tape wasn't going to yield to any amount of grunting and straining. I had nothing with which to pick the handcuff locks, even if the tape hadn't been in the way and I'd been double-jointed enough to get at them. There were various old tools and bits of junk on the shelves and scattered about the floor, and I might have found something to hack or rub the duct tape off—it would have been easy enough to get to my feet and hop over to the door and push the light switch on with my shoulder or my head—but even if I found a file or a hacksaw, I could never get enough leverage to cut through those handcuffs myself.

No doubt Houdini would have freed himself before Gamal and his buddy had finished locking up. And James Bond would have taken the hidden laser gun from his tie pin, burned his way out, unfolded the inflatable midget helicopter concealed in his jockstrap, pulled the tactical atomic missile from up his ass, and nuked the whole island out of existence while flying away with the woman with the big tits. I wasn't either of those guys. Ugly and vicious and even unsanitary as Gamal might be, he was right about my chances of going anywhere.

The reality was that I had no options. Until and unless something happened to alter the situation, there was nothing to be done.

So I did the one thing left: I went to sleep.

Which wasn't all that weird a thing to do; after all, I'd been up all night, and I was going to need every possible bit of metal and physical energy if any sort of break presented itself. I don't say I got to sleep easily, or slept all that well—the concrete floor was hard and cold, and there was no way to get comfortable tied up like that—but I slept.

They woke me up after awhile, opening the door, flicking on the light, the barrel of an AK-47 poking into the store-room while they checked me out. I didn't move or speak, and after a couple of minutes they went away and I went back to sleep.

And was awakened at last by the door banging open again, all the way this time, and light flooding into the storeroom. I rolled over onto my back, blinking at the dark silhouette in the brightly-lit doorway, as Gamal's voice said, "Here, Ferengi pig. Someone to keep you from being lonely."

A body came lurching through the doorway and fell heavily to the floor beside me. The door slammed shut, but not before I'd had a chance to recognize the face.

I said, "Cameron."

There was a groan and a wheezing sound. "Dane? Oh, shit, Dane." It was the voice of a man in great pain. "They shot me, Dane," Cameron said. "Couple of rounds in the guts, one in the leg. Kicked me around some, too. . . ."

His voice trailed off weakly. I said, "Don't try to talk."

"No. Things I got to tell you." I heard him shifting position. "What I came down here to tell you, Dane. Those bastards out there, they're Abdelkader's old bunch. That's why they want you. They know who you are, now."

My mind seemed to short out for a second. When I could speak again I said, "That's not possible, Cameron. They're not old enough—"

"Oh, they're not the original ones. Not what I mean," he said with an effort. "Guess they were just kids when you took him out. But they'd remember. They weren't that young. Christ, they start carrying a gun by eleven, twelve, you know that."

He paused, fighting for breath. "Probably grew up hearing about the martyr, sacred duty of revenge, all that shit. You got to get out of here, Dane," he said raggedly. "They're planning to take you back to Lebanon, hold a trial—probably torture you, try to get you to say you were working for the U.S. when you did it. Then they're gonna execute you."

Somebody seemed to be pushing a long icicle up my ass.

I said, "How did they find out—"

"Later." He coughed briefly, an ugly painful sound in the darkness. "Got to get out of here. Tell you while we're working on it. Don't think I've got much time. It's pretty bad."

I thought for a moment. "Hang on."

I worked my feet under me and stood up, almost falling. Hopping clumsily, navigating by memory and guess, I inched across the room until I bumped into something solid. My face felt the metal of the door. A little groping located the switch; I nuzzled at it until it snapped upward and light flooded the storeroom.

Cameron was lying on his side, his hands behind him, duct tape around his wrists. There was blood all over the front of his shirt and trousers. His face was white as chalk.

I hopped back over to him and started to bend down for a closer look, but he said impatiently, "Find something to cut the tape."

I pogoed over to the row of shelves and looked. There was a rusty but serviceable-looking handsaw sticking out, and I turned around and backed up to it and gripped the handle. Cameron was watching me. "Good," he said as I hopped back toward him. "Sit down. Get your back up close to mine."

I flopped awkwardly down behind him and rolled over, clutching the saw. A moment later I felt him pushing against the blade. "Hold it as solid as you can," he said.

The saw jerked and vibrated as Cameron dragged his taped wrists up and down the serrated blade. It shouldn't have taken more than a couple of passes, but Cameron was weak now. "Ah," he said finally. "Now let me have that thing."

I let go the saw and turned. Cameron had his hands free; bits of ragged duct tape still clung to his wrists. He'd cut himself a good deal, too, though under the circumstances he probably hadn't noticed. "They didn't bother with my feet," he said, "figured I was too shot up to do anything. Let me get you now."

I stuck out my legs; he cut the tape at my ankles with a few hacking strokes. As I turned back around I said, "I've got on cuffs under the tape."

"Huh. Well, let me get this shit off first." I heard him breathing heavily as he worked at the tape on my wrists with the saw. "All right," he said, and I heard him fall back onto the floor.

I stood up, feeling the prickling rush of circulation returning to half-numbed feet and ankles. Cameron was curled up, holding his stomach, his eyes closed. "Look around," he said without opening his eyes. "Find something to pick those cuffs. Piece of stiff wire or anything like that."

There didn't seem to be any wire in the place, except for bits of soft electrical wire that wouldn't work. I looked on all the shelves, finding nothing, till at last I noticed the pile of old bicycle parts. Sure enough, there were a few loose spokes lying on the floor.

"Perfect," Cameron said. His eyes were open again and his voice seemed a little stronger. "Some pliers too."

I found a pair of pliers and came back, holding everything behind me, while Cameron sat slowly and painfully up. "Right here," he said. "I used to be pretty good at this."

I watched as he took the pliers and bent the end of the bicycle spoke into a pick. "Ought to do," he muttered. "Simple-headed lock anyway. Turn around."

I felt him probing at the cuffs. "What you asked," he said, "I hate to tell you how they found out. Seems they been stalking Raintree for a good while, waiting for a chance to snatch him. In the process they—or rather their people around Washington—built up quite a collection of material on him. Photos, recordings, videotapes."

"Of Raintree with Brenda?"

He tugged at the cuffs. "Right. Turn your wrist this way . . . yeah, they got a lot of dirt while they were checking him out. So," he said, "when their snatch failed they fell back on an alternate plan. Maybe they had that in mind all along as a backstop."

I thought about it. "Blackmail?"

"Yeah." He was starting to wheeze again. "They got in touch with Raintree's office. Seems like they had some real weird stuff, too."

I nodded, remembering what I'd found in the bedroom. And Brenda had said something along those lines. . . . I said, "So where do I come into it?"

Cameron grunted. "Shit, I thought I had it that time. Well, either Raintree or his manager—I don't know which, there's a lot of lying going on right now—called up his good buddies at the Company and asked if they could do anything. The ragheads wanted more money than he could come up with, and a lot of other shit as well." Cameron coughed. "Like they wanted him to make this speech in Congress denouncing Israel . . . there." There was a click and I felt the metal fall away from my right wrist. "No need to waste time on the left, is there?"

I turned to look at him, rubbing my wrist. He was lying down again, looking bad. "Gimme your shirt," he said.

I skinned the sweaty T-shirt off over my head without asking what he wanted with it. He balled it up and pressed it against the holes in his stomach. "Slow down the leaks a little," he said. "So anyway, these Company honchos panicked. Somebody got the idea of making the ragheads a counteroffer. By now it was known who they were, and all the Company people involved knew about you and Abdelkader."

I realized suddenly what he was saying. "They made a trade?"

"Uh huh. The one thing these sons of bitches wanted more than anything in the world was the name and location of the guy who offed their little bush-league Ayatollah. They'd pass up everything else for that."

"So the Company sold me to get Raintree off the hook?"

"Not the Company. Just some highly-placed bastards in it." Cameron seemed to be having trouble breathing again. "Not high enough to get away with it, though. They got caught. Their necks are already on the block."

He closed his eyes again. "I was on my way to warn you," he said, "get you out of here, too damn late of course. Walked right into it. Came up from the dock, stopped and looked up at the house, and they shot me. The one in charge came out of the trailer and hollered at them for it. Then tried to find out who I was." He began coughing again. There was blood at the corners of his mouth now. "Didn't try very hard . . . probably figures to wait. . . ."

He drifted off somewhere, his face going slack, his hands still pressing the bloody shirt over his wounds. His chest was still going in and out, just barely.

I stood looking at him for a moment, wondering if there was anything I ought to be doing for him. My medical knowledge was extremely skimpy, but it was obvious he wasn't going to last much longer at this rate. The best thing I could do for him was to get both of us out of here; and I turned, finally, and went looking for the tools to do it with.

I was after weapons; there was no chance of cutting or digging through that steel door or the concrete-block walls in the time we had, though if there'd been a big sledgehammer I might have given it a shot. The only possibility was to jump the next man to open the door—and Ali was right; that sort of thing looks much easier in the movies.

There was quite an assortment of potentially lethal hardware on the premises—screwdrivers, a hammer, a shovel, even an axe—but it all required getting within arm's reach of the intended victim. I didn't think I was going to be able to do that. There was no place to hide anywhere near the door, and these people weren't going to fall for any of the old gags—lying on the floor and groaning, or playing dead—that sometimes fool unwary types into coming close and bending over a prisoner. I hefted the axe experimentally, wondering if I could throw it accurately enough to hit a man standing in the doorway. The ceiling was probably too low. . . .

I found myself staring at a flat red-and-white can on the top shelf, jammed way back in the corner. The label read:

FFFg

SUPER FINE

BLACK POWDER

DANGER—EXPLOSIVE

The powder for the cap-and-ball pistol, of course; I'd clean forgotten about it. I took it down carefully, thinking of various possibilities. "Look what we have here," I said to Cameron, but he didn't reply. He seemed to be unconscious.

I stood for a moment holding the can, playing out different scenarios in my head. Blow a hole in the wall? Probably possible, but a good chance I'd kill both of us in the process; and even if we survived the blast, Ali's men would be all over us before we could get to cover. Make some sort of grenade and throw it at whoever came in the door?

Then I saw the big red bicycle pump leaning against the wall.

I pulled the wrecked bicycle aside and dragged the pump out. It was an old-fashioned vertical tire pump, the kind you bend over and pump with both hands, not one of those little jobs they clip onto the frame. It was dirty and rusty and its hose was missing, but that was immaterial for my purposes.

I found a pipe wrench and unscrewed the top end, removing the handle and the plunger, leaving me with a length of two-inch pipe about three feet long, with a heavy iron casting closing one end. It felt pretty solid. I hoped Schwinn had used good metal.

There didn't seem to be any accurate way to calculate the charge; I just held the thing up and poured what seemed like a reasonable amount of black powder down its throat, and then a little more on top of that. I ripped a bit of denim from my pants leg and used that as a wad to hold the powder in place, tamping it down with the pump plunger.

There was no shortage of possible projectiles. The lead balls for the .44 were at the house, but the shelves and the floor provided a liberal supply of rusty old bolts, nails, nuts, and unidentifiable bits of scrap metal, even a few steel bearing balls. I dumped it all in until it felt like enough, shoved another rag down the bore to keep it all down tight against the powder, and laid the whole package very carefully on a shelf for the moment.

An old splintery wooden box made an adequate mount, with the addition of a few odds and ends to get the right upward angle. I tinkered with things for a few minutes until the barrel of my cannon seemed to be pointed roughly at the upper half of the doorway. I didn't think precise accuracy was going to be a problem here, but I was, after all, only going to get one try.

There was an opening in the cast-iron base where the hose fitting had been. I trickled more black powder into that, letting it mound up a bit on top, and then screwed the cap tightly back onto the powder can—I didn't know, but I suspected even one spark would set the whole thing off—and replaced it on its shelf in the far corner.

I said, "Cameron? You got a lighter on you?"

He didn't reply. I went over and saw that he was very still. I touched the side of his neck, feeling for a pulse.

After a moment I took my hand away. Cameron wasn't going to make his retirement after all. Or maybe he just had.

I rolled him over and went through his pockets. If they'd taken his lighter I'd gone through all this for nothing, though I might be able to do something with the percussion caps . . . but it was there, in his pants pocket, covered with blood. Maybe that had discouraged any careful search. A crumpled pack in his shirt pocket contained a couple of bent Marlboros.

I looked down at him for a minute, feeling as if I ought to say something, but there was nothing that came to mind. His eyes were already closed. There was really only one thing I could do for him now.

I went over and flipped the light off and felt my way back in the dark, moving very carefully, and sat down beside my improvised artillery piece, holding the lighter and the cigarettes. You may fire when you are ready, Gridley. . . .

It wasn't all that long, I suppose; but sitting there in the dark, not daring to move, time did tend to pass at a pretty leisurely pace.

And at that I came close to blowing it; the heavy steel door muffled the sound of the padlock snapping open, and I barely managed to thumb the lighter and set fire to the cigarette between my lips before the door boomed open and a single figure stepped into the rectangle of light. A voice called out something, sounding angry or surprised.

I didn't wait to find out which. I mashed the glowing end of the cigarette into the mound of black powder over the touchole, saw a quick flash of red as the first grains ignited, and hurled myself to one side as the world blew up.

12

· · · · ·

THE BLAST WAS ENORMOUS IN THE CONFINED space, far louder than I had expected. There was a great red flash and the room filled with dense choking smoke. Something sang past my ear and whanged off the wall nearby.

Deafened and half-blind, I lunged through the smoke toward the doorway. Out of the corner of my eye I saw that my cannon had peeled back on itself like a banana, the shiny ends of split metal jagged and sharp. Too much powder, I thought dazedly. Wonder I didn't blow myself to shit.

There was no one standing in the doorway now. When I looked outside, though, I saw him lying on the ground. What there was of him, anyway. Gamal had found the ultimate solution to unsightly facial hair: he didn't have a face any more. Or much of a head, for that matter. Poor Gamal; he hadn't been very pretty even when he was alive, but he really looked like hell now.

But the AK-47 lying beside him was just about as beautiful a sight as I'd seen lately.

I grabbed it up, checked quickly to make sure it was undamaged, and flicked the selector lever to single-shot just as a man came out on the deck of the house, shouting and pointing a rifle at me. He made a dead easy target.

I laid the sights on him and fired twice and he dropped his weapon, took one step forward, folded slowly over the railing, and pitched headfirst into space. I couldn't see him hit the ground from where I stood, but I heard the soft loose thud his body made on the sand.

I wanted to search Gamal's body for ammunition, but things were starting to get busy. Another man appeared on the deck; I shot at him but he ducked back around the corner of the house and fired back at me. A bare-chested figure came charging around the end of the trailer, holding a gun. I fired twice from waist level, pointing rather than aiming. He stopped as if he had run into a clothesline, turned half around, and fell in a heap.

By now gunfire was coming from several directions, a little wild so far but rapidly getting closer. A bullet went *bweeowww* off the concrete wall, much too close to my head. Clearly time to relocate. I turned and sprinted around the end of the blockhouse and, using the building for cover, ran for the shelter of the dunes.

Behind me, above the gunfire, I heard Ali's voice calling for someone to go down and sink the American's boat. That would be the one Cameron had arrived in; Ali wasn't taking any chances on my getting off the island.

Down near the boat dock somebody responded by cranking off what sounded like most of a magazine of 7.62mm. Billy Jumper would be out one boat. If I got out of this alive I'd buy him a new one.

Sweat stinging my eyes, grasses slapping at my arms and legs, feet struggling for purchase in the soft sand, I ran through the dunes. Behind me the shouting faded to unintelligibility. From the position of the sun I estimated it must be the middle of the afternoon, perhaps three or four.

Out of the few possible directions to run, only one offered

even an inside-straight chance at survival. I headed south, toward the narrow waist of the island.

It took them a surprisingly long time to come after me. Maybe one of the men I'd shot hadn't died immediately and they'd tried to save him, though I couldn't picture this bunch wasting much time on humanitarian concerns. Maybe they got into an argument about the tactics to be followed. Most likely they were just being careful, taking their time. They knew I wasn't going anywhere; and, until the plane came in the evening, neither were they.

The situation was several degrees worse than impossible for me. Offhand, I couldn't recall being in a worse tactical setup. There were four of them left, with automatic rifles. That was more than enough to pin me down and cover each other while they surrounded me and smoked me out of whatever cover I might find. And I was fairly sure they'd abandoned any serious intention of taking me alive again, though Ali might still give it a shot if the opportunity presented itself.

I could have coped with the odds—had coped with worse, more than once—if that had been the only problem, but it wasn't. The terrain was appalling, from my point of view. There wasn't one square foot of ground on the island that wouldn't hold a big and obvious footprint. Wherever I went, they could track me with no trouble at all; you don't have to be an Apache scout to follow prints in soft sand.

There was little real cover. The dunes were fine as far as they went, but four or even two men could easily flank a dune on both sides and flush a man out. The sea-oats and other grasses rarely grew thick enough to hide a man, and the clumps of live-oaks were small and far between. And the island itself was so narrow, and most of its surface so exposed, that four men could simply spread out and work their way from end to end and be almost sure of flushing any living thing bigger than a crab. If I managed to hide or somehow slip between them once, they'd get me on the next sweep, or the next.

I might have been able to play games with them until dark—it was a long time, but not impossibly long—and then they might have said the hell with it and flown away, figuring to get me another time. I didn't really think so, after they'd lost five men to me—to say nothing of their late spiritual leader—but it didn't matter. I didn't want them leaving here alive. I wasn't going to spend the next few weeks, or months, or years, looking over my shoulder; finish it here and now, one way or the other. . . .

I paused long enough to drink deeply from a reed-grown rainwater pool—Chuck Norris or Bruce Lee would have dived in and lain there breathing through a hollow reed, but then they had scripts that guaranteed the bad guys were morons—and chugged on down the center of the island, making no attempt to conceal my tracks. The sun was hot on my shirtless back. My stomach was beginning to complain bitterly that it hadn't been fed in a very long time.

Down at the narrow neck of sand that connected the halves of the island, I paused to consider the half-wrecked picnic tables and benches that still lay where Ray and the gang had left them. A man just might be able to use that picnic-table top as a raft. He'd never get out of rifle shot of the island before being spotted and killed, but I filed the idea away for possible use after dark in case things went completely to hell.

I found myself a good spot just below the cove, sheltered by a pair of big live-oaks, with a view of the entire sandy neck. At the narrowest point there was nothing growing, not even grasses. If they wanted me they'd have to come that way. I snuggled myself down into the sand, among the gnarled roots of the live-oaks, and trained the Kalashnikov on the naked spot, and waited.

I had more of a wait than I'd expected. That was all right; it let my pulse and breathing slow to normal. The flocks of long-legged sea birds got over the disturbance of my passage and returned to the beach, stalking up and down, hunched over like Groucho Marx. The only sound was the wind and the hiss of the outgoing tide.

When they finally came they did it so slowly and quietly that I might not have spotted them right away; but there were keener eyes and ears than mine on the scene, and the sea birds took off in a great squawking cloud minutes before I saw the head and shoulders of a man moving cautiously into view above the tops of a row of sea-oats. A second later another man ran quietly from behind a dune and dived behind a live-oak.

I couldn't quite identify anyone at this distance, which was too bad. I wanted Ahmad if I could get him, because he was clearly the smartest one of the bunch. One of the basic problems of that kind of fighting is that the stupidest people on the other side tend to get killed first, instead of the clever bastards you'd rather eliminate. But then I recognized Ali moving from cover to cover; he was the only one with no shirt on, and even at this range I could see that massive chest.

They all stopped and ducked down out of sight as they approached the narrow place; I could hear indistinct voices as they discussed the problem. Crazy or not, they were Arab guerrilla fighters with years of experience; they knew all about the consequences of advancing across open sand against automatic-weapons fire.

Ali was no coward, whatever his other shortcomings; he was the one, finally, who tried it. He came from behind the live-oaks, down in a deep crouch, running fast across the sandy neck; I hung the sights on him and triggered as he reached the middle.

I'd have had him if I hadn't forgotten to push the selector to full-automatic fire. The Kalashnikov banged once and Ali spun around, clutched the side of his hip, and started back toward the live-oaks. I cursed and flipped the lever to full-auto and sighted again. The shadows under the live-oaks lit up with muzzle flashes and a storm of bullets lashed into the trees around me; bark flew in all directions and I ducked. When I raised my head again Ali was nowhere to be seen.

I didn't think I'd hurt him very badly. Maybe it would slow him down a trifle, but I was going to have to do a lot better than that.

Things were quiet for a little while. I lay there under the live-oaks and imagined the conference that must be making place over on the other side of the narrows. They knew where I was now, but how to get at me without crossing that lethal open space? They were too professional to waste ammunition taking blind potshots at me when they couldn't see me; I considered trying a few bursts to draw them out, but I had only what was left in the one magazine.

When they did open up, I knew somebody must be making a move. There were at least three automatic weapons laying down fire on my position; the air was full of popping bullets and flying bark and sprays of sand, and a few small limbs splintered and fell nearby. I got my head up several times, just barely enough to get a look at the open ground, but I didn't see anyone moving, and the fire was too heavy for an extended scan. Splinters rained down onto my bare back. A slug thumped into a root no more than a foot from my face.

Then, just as suddenly, the fire stopped, as if someone had turned off a faucet. The silence was deafening.

It could only mean one thing: whoever they were covering had gotten across. They'd ceased fire because they had a man in the area and they didn't want to hit him.

I lay absolutely still listening.

He was good; I almost didn't hear him at all. The wind and the sea sounds masked the tiny crush of his feet on the sand, and he was taking his time, moving with great care. I'm not even sure what it was that gave him away—a stalk of grass, perhaps, scratching across fabric, or the slight creak of a rifle sling. Maybe I just felt him coming.

I set the AK-47 on safety and eased back from the trees, crawling to the cover of a clump of sea-oats and then down between a couple of low dunes, straightening up when the dunes hid me, moving down toward the beach. I saw the tracks before I saw him, coming up out of the water, pointed inland; he'd waded across the cove, while his colleagues kept me too busy to look that way, and come up across the beach to take me from the flank. It had been a gutsy move; if I'd spotted him out there in the water he'd have been a dead man.

I moved cautiously around the hump of the dune, watching the line of tracks that disappeared up between this dune and the next. A second later I saw him, climbing silently toward the place where I had been. His back was to me.

I wished momentarily for a knife; I'd have been willing to try to take him out silently, so Ali and the others would have to wonder a little longer. The AK-47, unfortunately, didn't have the little folding bayonet under the barrel, that we used to see in Nam. I gave a quarter-second's thought to jumping him and killing him with my hands, but that was too crazy; and he'd probably get a shot off anyway.

He stopped halfway up the side of the dune. In a moment he was going to look around; somehow he'd heard or felt something. I slipped the selector lever to single-shot and laid the sights on the back of his head and squeezed.

His skull seemed to bulge with the impact. He went completely slack, all at once, dead before he even started to fall.

I ran toward the body, knowing I didn't have time to waste but feeling an acute need for ammunition. I turned him over, searching. The bullet had blown a good deal of his face off on its way out. It wasn't Ali, though, or Ahmad; the body wasn't big enough. It wasn't skinny enough to be Zaal either. It was somebody I hadn't met socially at all. I was a little bit surprised, and disappointed. I'd figured it had to be Ahmad.

This one hadn't carried any extra ammo—probably they'd all come running when I blew Gamal away, with whatever they happened to have on them—but I yanked the magazine out of his rifle and stuck it in my belt. From the weight it seemed to be better than half full. I threw his rifle into the water and clambered up to the crest of the dune just in time to see the others running across the sandy neck toward the place where I'd been.

I snapped off a full-auto burst, but I couldn't tell if I hit anything. I didn't think so; they'd been across and almost to cover before I fired. I dropped back down out of sight as a burst of fire kicked sand from the crest of the dune.

So now they were on my side of the isthmus. And now it was three to one, but that was still a little steep. . . .

And they were going to have me nailed in a few minutes; the tactical situation had just been turned around. All they had to do was circle around and push me back toward the beach or toward the open neck they'd just crossed; there was no real cover between where I stood and the interior of the southern half of the island. They wouldn't take long figuring it out, either.

I tried to visualize where they must be and what they'd be doing. They'd follow my tracks down between the dunes and then around toward their dead pal; it was the obvious route. But they'd leave one man up at the top to cover them, in case I'd doubled back to escape or bushwhack them.

For a moment I closed my eyes, trying to remember the exact shape of the terrain, trying to get inside their heads, to see the scene from their perspective. If I was right, there was one obvious place to post the covering man. If I was wrong, or if it wasn't obvious to them—but then I'd run out of alternatives and options.

I worked my way up the sandy slope again, angling off to the right, moving as fast as I could in the loose sliding sand, flattening out and crawling the last couple of feet like a lizard. All my internal muscles contracted as I eased my head up and looked through the sea-oats.

He was standing there, all right, not precisely where I'd calculated but close enough. It was Zaal; there was no mistaking that spider-skinny shape. He was holding his weapon ready, his finger on the trigger, and his head turned slowly and steadily to scan the surrounding ground. In another second he'd be looking straight at me.

There was a sudden shout from down on the other side of my dune. They'd found the most recent casualty. Zaal's head snapped back around; he took a step forward.

I came up on my knees and pushed the Kalashnikov's barrel through the sea-oats and fired, aiming deliberately for the lower body, putting the whole burst into the area between belt and crotch.

Zaal's body jerked upright, then began to curl forward. His mouth opened and a high-pitched scream began to rise above the sound of the wind and the sea. He dropped the rifle; his hands came up and clutched at the front of his pants. He fell to his knees.

I didn't watch any longer. I ran down the dune, great wild steps, sinking in up to my ankles, and took off along the beach. If Ali or Ahmad had the cold presence of mind to ignore Zaal for the moment and run on down to the beach, they could gun me down like a duck in a shooting gallery; but I was betting the whole roll that nobody, not even those two, could ignore those screams. The screaming was much louder now. It was a sound for a nightmare, and it went on and on.

I nearly made it. I was clear across the narrow open stretch, a long jump from the cover of the live-oaks, when the shots sounded behind me. Sand kicked up on all sides and bullets cut the sea-oats. Something jabbed me in the side, not painfully, more like a hard prod from a rude forefinger. I knew instantly what it was; I'd felt it before, and you never forget it.

The impact spun me around and made me stumble; that was probably the thing that saved my life, as the rest of the burst popped nastily through the place where I'd been. I flopped forward into the shade of the nearest live-oak, rolling to one side, feeling a growing burning in my side as the damaged nerve-ends began to register what had happened. Ahmad was standing at the top of a dune, firing from the shoulder. Even over the gunfire I could hear Zaal's terrible screaming.

I brought the AK-47 up and let off a long burst, firing fast without aiming. Ahmad dropped out of sight. I was pretty sure I hadn't hit him. Sure enough, a moment later he popped up long enough to rake the live-oaks with a return burst.

All the same, nobody was going to be in a hurry to come after me across that open stretch. I laid the rifle aside and had a look at the damage.

It could have been a lot worse. Only one bullet had hit me, and it had come close to missing me altogether. As best I could tell from a cautious examination, it had hit me from behind, low on the left side, and punched on through and out the front. It hadn't done any nasty tricks like tumbling or fragmenting. It had just drilled a simple hole that didn't seem to have touched any major organs.

It was, on the other hand, bleeding profusely. I couldn't stay here and wait for Ali and Ahmad to give me a shot at them, as I'd intended. Eventually I'd get weak and dizzy from loss of blood—the heat, and an empty stomach, wouldn't help—and then I wouldn't be able to shoot or think straight.

I managed to rip another piece from the remains of my jeans and I held that in place over the exit wound, which seemed to be bleeding more than the entry hole. It wasn't good enough by any means, but it would have to do for now. I took my belt off and wrapped it around myself and cinched it tight over the wounds, nearly passing out from the momentary pain; then I got to my feet, loosed off one more burst in the enemy's general direction just to keep them honest, and set off back toward the north end of the island.

I kept telling myself it was only about a mile. It still felt like clear across Hell and half of Texas. By the time I was halfway there I was starting to stumble and weave; once I nearly dropped the AK-47. My stomach wanted to heave, but there was nothing in it to heave. It felt as if somebody had a hot soldering iron rammed through my side. My half-assed attempt at a bandage hadn't been worth the trouble of rigging it up; the blood was running freely down my side and soaking my pants.

For the moment, at least, nobody seemed to be close on my trail. Give the sons of bitches that much credit; they'd stayed with Zaal. I'd been half certain they'd go off and leave him, or simply shoot him. In fact I wasn't sure I wouldn't have shot him myself, in their situation.

Well, whatever else happened, one tomcat spirit would rest a little better now.

I didn't think I'd bought myself much time, though. Zaal wasn't going to last all that long.

But now I could see the white house rising above the trees up ahead, and the sight gave me a burst of new energy. I staggered on through the tall grasses, past the live-oaks and around the end of the blockhouse—Gamal was still lying where he'd fallen—and a moment later I was inside the trailer.

They hadn't made that big a mess of the place; it wasn't much worse than I'd let it get a few times. I stepped over some broken dishes, kicked some wadded-up clothing out of my way, and went into the bathroom. The mirror had been smashed on the medicine chest, but the contents were still there.

There were no gauze pads big enough to do the job; I ripped pieces from a sheet and taped them in place, running the tape clear around me to hold it tightly. I wasn't worried about sterility; if I wasn't off this island and in professional hands long before infection had time to set in, it wouldn't matter.

Back in the front room, I thought about trying to eat something, but the idea alone was enough to make me gag. Instead I got a bottle of Jim Beam from the cupboard—none of the booze had been touched; Ali's boys were good enough Muslims to leave it alone—and took a long pull. The first swallow hit bottom and instantly tried to come back up, but the second went down better, and the third was downright smooth.

I set the bottle down and moved toward the door. The whisky was enough to kick my abused internal machinery over a little longer, but one more drink and I'd start to fade. If Ali and Ahmad had sense enough to simply sit down and wait a couple of hours, they could come get me without much trouble at all.

I stepped outside, holding the AK-47 in one hand, muzzle upward, while I steadied myself against the trailer with the other hand. The sun was starting to dip toward the distant Texas plain. Somewhere in the distance there was a deep droning sound, not yet loud but growing. That meant something important, but my mind wasn't computing very well. I walked around the end of the trailer and almost bumped into Ahmad.

He was up against the wall of the trailer, moving sideways; he must have been in the process of trying to creep up on me. His rifle was held across his chest, the muzzle pointing past his left shoulder. His eyes went round when he saw me; his mouth dropped open.

I don't think I reacted faster than Ahmad; I think my weapon just had a shorter distance to travel. I snapped the Kalashnikov's muzzle downward, squeezing the trigger as I did so, holding the trigger down and letting the full-auto burst walk through him, head and chest and belly. I probably killed him ten or fifteen times before the AK-47 snapped empty. The range was so close the muzzle flash lit up his face.

He slid down the trailer wall—the metal behind him was perforated with a lot of new holes; I thought abstractedly that this trailer was going to need a lot of work—and I dumped the empty magazine out of the rifle and reached for the one in my belt.

Except that there wasn't a magazine in my belt. I'd lost it somewhere, probably back where I got hit or while I was trying to stop the leaks in my side.

I started to turn, to go back and look for a loaded weapon or a fresh magazine on one of the dead. But a voice said, "Dane!"

Ali stepped out from behind the nearest live-oak. He wasn't grinning now. He looked bad. I noticed that his pants leg was bloody. Must have hit him a little better than I'd thought.

The AK-47 in his hands, however, was rock steady as he held it trained on my chest.

He said in Arabic, "So it has come to this, Dane. Abdelkader is dead, all my men are dead."

The droning sound was getting loud now. It was definitely coming this way. Ali didn't seem to notice.

"Now," he said, "you too are dead."

He raised the AK-47 to his shoulder. There was a tiny twanging sound and then a kind of soft thump. Ali stopped moving for a moment, a deeply puzzled expression on his face.

The AK-47's muzzle dropped. There was a brief burst of noise as a couple of rounds went off into the sand. Then the rifle fell, while Ali slowly lowered his head and stared in amazement at the steel point of the arrow that had emerged through the center of his chest.

He looked up at me, as if he wanted to say something; his mouth opened. But all that came out was a rattling croak and then a gush of blood. A second later he fell forward on his face.

Billy Jumper came out from behind a tree. He had a bow in his hand.

"You all right?" he called. Then, as he walked toward me, "Hey, Dane, you been shot?"

I leaned against the trailer. "It's not serious. Looks worse than it is."

"That Cameron went out there today," he said. "I heard a few shots, didn't think much of it, figured it was just you practicing or something. Then he didn't come back, then there was all this heavy shooting going on, I knew something bad was wrong. Wasted a lot of time trying to get the sheriff's office to do something, they gave me this crap about secret government maneuvers. Finally decided I better come take care of it myself. Came in at low speed so they wouldn't hear me. Sorry I took so long."

He went over and looked down at Ali's body for a long time. The arrow shaft stuck out between the bare shoulder blades, the gray-barred turkey-feather vanes fluttering slightly in the wind.

His face contorted oddly; it looked as if he was trying not to cry. "Hell," he said suddenly.

He turned and straightened, all in one abrupt movement, throwing the bow hard into the waving sea-oats. He walked past me, not looking at me, and sat down in one of the folding chairs and put his head in his hands.

The drone was a roar and now I came awake, grabbing up Ahmad's rifle from the sand, running painfully across the open ground and down the wooden walkway as the seaplane bellowed past just above the treetops. I heard it start to turn, heading into the wind to land. Now I could see it settling toward the water, its spinning propellers catching the setting sun. I didn't recognize the make.

I was hoping they'd come on in, taxi up to the dock, let me get a clear shot at the pilot and then Ishak if he tried to get out . . . and for a minute it looked as if it might go down that way, as the pilot cut power and the graceful blue boat-shaped hull started to touch down amid the waves. The water was maybe a tiny bit rough, just then, but not dangerously so; I'd seen seaplanes land in much worse. I stood in the shadows and tried to be inconspicuous.

But somebody had seen something, I guess; or maybe there was a signal somebody was supposed to make from the island, or maybe the pilot just got spooked. Suddenly the engine note rose again and the seaplane began to lift.

I said, "Son of a *bitch*," and ran out onto the dock and aimed the AK-47 at the seaplane and opened fire.

There was, of course, no chance in hell of actually shooting the damn thing down. A hundred men shooting at once might bring down an occasional airplane with small-arms fire; one man, except in comic books, isn't going to do anything of the sort. And I knew it; I was just letting off frustration and rage. If I hadn't had the rifle I'd probably have thrown a damn rock.

And I don't really believe I hit the airplane, though the range wasn't all that long and it was coming straight toward me. More likely the pilot simply saw me shooting at him and panicked for a second. At that altitude, with so little flying speed, a second was more than enough.

The left wingtip dipped sharply. The nose started to rise. The float at the end of the left wing dug into the crest of a wave.

I let the empty rifle fall to the dock at my feet. I knew what was going to happen next; I'd seen something like it once before, years ago, on the Mediterranean. It had the inevitability of an avalanche.

The float struts crumpled. The left wingtip struck the water. The seaplane lifted and then went into a kind of lazy cartwheel. The noise was tremendous. Pieces flew off. The whole thing struck the water and disappeared in an enormous fountain of spray. When the sheets of water fell back I could see the seaplane's tail and part of one wing sticking up above the surface for a moment, but then that too sank out of sight.

I watched for a few minutes just in case somebody got out. Nobody did.

I walked back up to the house. Billy Jumper appeared, a look of concern on his wrinkled brown face. "Sorry I lost it for a minute there," he said. "My boat's beached over yonder. Come on. We got to get you to a doctor."

He looked around at the scene. "I don't think I'm going to ask," he said. "I don't think I want to know."

13
· · · · ·

THE COMPANY FLEW ME BACK TO WASHINGTON; not that there was anything wrong with me that couldn't have been handled by any competent emergency-room intern, but they wanted to ask me some questions. I got the impression that they were also concerned that I might answer the wrong questions from the wrong people.

There was a man who came to see me at my hotel room. He was a big, heavy-set, gray-haired man somewhere in his late fifties or early sixties; he had hound-dog bags under his eyes and a snapping-turtle mouth. He said his name was Griner.

It turned out that he wanted to know about Cameron.

"We worked together a lot of years," he said. "We were in the old Occupation Army in Germany, before we both went into the Company." He made the barest sound of a laugh. "Did you know that Military Intelligence in Munich used to be in an old hotel called the Eye of God? The sign was still up over the door when we were there."

He leaned forward and looked at me with eyes that didn't look to have seen a lot to laugh about lately. "This is an unofficial visit, Dane," he said. "You don't have to talk to me at all. I just wanted to know how it was for him, at the end."

So I told him the whole story. He nodded here and there and made a couple of grunts that might have been surprise, but he didn't speak until I was done.

"So old Frank went out giving it his best shot," he said then. "That's good to know."

"If it hadn't been for him," I said, "I'd have been dead by now."

"Ah." He nodded again, heavily. "Well, I'm glad his death didn't go completely for nothing."

He sat back; he seemed to be coming to a decision. "You understand," he said, "this whole conversation never took place. In fact I've never even met you."

I said, "I don't even see you right now."

"Good. They've clamped the lid down, you see. The whole thing's under highest-level classification, need-to-know only—and they don't think very many people need to know. This wasn't really one of the Company's more shining moments. We aren't supposed to be in bed with Congressmen." He made a face. "Unfortunate choice of words, under the circumstances, but. . . ."

He stood up. "I just thought you might like to know," he said, "that the persons within the Company who sold you out have experienced some major career adjustments in the last few days. I don't suppose you find that adequate—I wouldn't, in your shoes—but it's better than nothing."

He cleared his throat. "There's a certain apprehension in some quarters that you might decide to take some sort of retaliatory action on your own. In view of your, well, specialized talents."

I shrugged. "I thought about it. But the hell with it. I'm tired of the whole thing."

"Thought you might be." He started to turn toward the door, stopped, turned back again. "One thing. Jerry Raintree."

"Ah, yes. The good Congressman," I said. "How is he these days? We used to be so close."

Griner ignored my half-assed sarcasm. "He wasn't in on any of it, Dane," he said seriously. "He knew about the blackmail attempt, knew they'd turned the matter over to his contacts in the Company, but I guarantee you he never knew, until it was too late, what sort of deal they'd made."

I thought it over. It was nice of him to tell me; it was even possible he was telling the truth. But I didn't see that it made a lot of difference now.

"He was pretty upset when he did find out," Griner said. "Really raised hell."

He must have gotten over it, then; Representative Raintree never did call or come by to express his indignation to me personally. Or if he did I was out.

After the doctors were done doctoring and the debriefers were done debriefing me, and various other Company employees ran out of questions for the time being, I decided there was something I wanted to do before I left town. I'd been thinking about it for awhile.

It took me a couple of days; I had to make a lot of calls, go see some old acquaintances, call in a few favors. Maybe a couple of times I might have gotten pretty close to the definition of blackmail, if you wanted to be tiresome about it. It wasn't just a matter of picking other people's brains and getting unauthorized access to information, though. I had to make connections, figure out how Fact A hooked up with Fact B in order to know how to word Question C and who might have the answer. It had been a long time since I'd done that sort of work; there was almost a nostalgic feel to it.

Of course, I could have done more of the work myself, gotten it done faster, if I'd been even halfway competent with computers. I had a suspicion there were twelve-year-old hackers around the country who could have found out what I wanted to know in a couple of easy hours on their little home hookups. Every time I get around computer people, I feel like I ought to walk on my knuckles.

I found what I was after, though, in the end. After all, it wasn't some big military secret; it was just a phone number and an address up in Silver Spring, Maryland. Silver Spring? For some reason I'd been expecting Georgetown.

I tried calling a few times, but there was no answer. At last I got impatient, rented a little Japanese car with clunky suspension and absolutely no power under the hood, and went for a drive.

Finding the address took a little more asking around once I got to Silver Spring. It turned out to be in a relatively new development, all winding streets and little look-alike houses, most of the lawns still trying to get started. That was another surprise; I'd pictured an apartment, something modern and hip-looking, maybe one of those condominium setups. Life-style stereotypes, I guess. The number I had was a small white house at the end of a curving dead-end street. There was a car parked in the open carport.

I walked up the little front walk, the still-new concrete rough under my shoes. The hole in my side was hurting a bit from the drive. I was supposed to go back over to Langley tomorrow and let the doctor make sure it was healing properly. I stepped up onto the pool-table-sized front porch and pushed the doorbell button.

And after a few minutes, pushed again, and then again; but there was no response, no sound except that of the air conditioner running.

Well, so much for that. Had myself a drive, out of pocket a few bucks, for nothing but a look at a nondescript white cottage. I didn't even have a pen or paper with me to leave a note.

I walked around to the carport, out of mere idle curiosity. The car was a neat-looking little American-made compact, dark blue and nearly new, with Maryland tags. I wondered why it was sitting here with nobody home, but there were a hundred possible explanations for that.

Irritated with myself now, I went back up and hit the button once more, and then knocked hard just in case the doorbell was broken. Still no answer; but then I got to looking at the door.

I wasn't a cop or a detective and never had been. All the same, I'd had a certain amount of training, years ago, and when you live a certain life you better get in the habit of noticing these things. The door had been opened, at least once and not a long time ago, by somebody who hadn't used keys. "Signs of forced entry" would have been putting it a bit too strongly; there were only a few little things—scratches on the brass, small chipped places in the paint of the door and its frame—but they added up to a very clear picture.

And, of course, there could be plenty of explanations of that too: keys lost or locked inside, a helpful neighbor coming over with a pry bar.

But there was the car sitting there; and there was the bad feeling that was starting to erect the hairs on my forearms.

I started to try the door myself, but then I stopped and looked around. There didn't seem to be anyone in sight along the little stub of a dead-end street; everyone was most likely at work, the kids in daycare centers. It took a two-job family, I guessed, to pay for one of these houses nowadays, unless you had some kind of special angle. I didn't think anyone was watching. All the same, I didn't want to be seen going in the front way if something more discreet was available.

I stepped off the porch and walked quickly around to the back. The rear screen wasn't hooked, and the back door yielded soon enough to a little persuasion. I looked around once more and stepped inside.

The air conditioner was turned way up; the place was like a meat locker. That was my first and strongest impression, how chilly it was. Which could only mean that nobody had been opening doors for a day or two at least; and who goes off on a trip and leaves the air conditioner cranked up to full ice-age chill, with electric bills what they are? This was looking worse and worse. And the lights, I saw, were on in the living room.

The interior of the house was simply and even sparsely furnished, all modern metal and glass stuff, no potted plants in sight, very little decoration. The kitchen featured an expensive-looking microwave. On the living-room wall hung a large abstract painting, big wipes and smears of bright primary colors, pretty idiotic as art but pleasant enough as wallpaper. I really wasn't paying much attention to the decor or the furnishings by now.

I found her in the bedroom. Later it occurred to me that there was something appropriate about that.

She'd been working unsuccessfully on a tan the last time I'd seen her, and she still hadn't made any progress. Her skin was paler than pale now, a bloodless papery white that was starting to turn here and there to dull bluish shades of gray.

She lay across the bed, on her back, one foot resting on the floor. She'd had on a long flower-print robe, but it had fallen open and she wore nothing underneath. A towel lay on the floor; the bathroom door was open and a light was on. I guessed she'd been coming from a bath, or maybe getting ready to take one, when they came in. The sound of the shower or tub running could have covered their entry. That actually works, not just in the movies where they do it to have an excuse for a nude shot.

They—I don't know why I kept thinking of "they"; it could as easily have been a single man, or woman—had shot her twice through the heart. The two small bluish holes between those incredible breasts could have been covered by a child's hand. The sheets beneath her were soaked with blood, now dried to an ugly rust-colored crust. Her eyes were open, but her face showed no particular expression. After rigor mortis passes, everything goes slack; only the freshly dead have that look of surprise.

She'd been lying there awhile, a couple of days at least, or so I judged from the overall skin color. It hadn't been long enough for serious decomposition to set in, but there was a definite odor in the air; the biological processes were at work. The air conditioning had slowed things down. I couldn't guess by how much. I didn't want to think what she'd have looked like, in the heat of a Maryland summer, if the air conditioner had quit.

I stood there looking at her for a few minutes, not touching her, not moving closer than the doorway. Poor Brenda. She'd wanted to be a material girl and she'd run up against certain realities of the material world. The cold hard facts of life, Porter Wagoner would have called it. I hoped they'd shot her quickly, before she had time to register what was going to happen to her. I didn't want her to have ended in terror.

It was strange; I hadn't ever known her well, still didn't know much about her. We hadn't, God knows, been in love or anything close to it; if you nailed it down to absolute truth, we hadn't even liked each other all that well in a lot of ways. We'd just helped each other get through a couple of nights, played an adult version of Doctor. I'll let you use mine if you'll let me use yours. . . . I wasn't even sure why I'd come looking for her.

So why did it cut me up so badly seeing her dead like that? I felt as if all my insides had been removed and there was a big empty place in the middle of my body.

Maybe it was just the damn cruel waste of it all—not just Brenda, but Cameron and all the rest of it, all the way back to Abdelkader and beyond. Maybe it was just catching up to me.

I didn't waste time searching for clues or evidence. I wouldn't have known how, and if I'd found anything, there was nothing I could have done with it. There were other people who got paid to take care of such things. I went out the way I'd come in, being careful not to touch or move anything, and drove away.

It took a few minutes of driving around to find an outdoor pay phone where I wasn't likely to be overheard. I dialed a certain number I wasn't supposed to have, and when a woman answered I gave her a code I wasn't authorized to know or use. After a bit more diddling around I got Griner on the line.

I said, "There is a dead woman in a house in Silver Spring. She's been shot."

There was a pause, just a couple of seconds, and then Griner said slowly, "This person—you're referring to a certain woman who was, um, involved in recent events?"

"You've got it." I gave him the address. He could have gotten it easily enough from the same source I had, and with a lot less trouble, but I figured it would save time.

He said, "How long has she been dead?"

"Looks like at least a couple of days, maybe more."

"Professional hit?"

"If I've ever seen one."

And God knows you have. I could hear him thinking it, clear across the long-distance connection.

"Are you going to be there?" he asked.

"Christ, no. And I didn't leave any tracks. Better get the boys with the big broom," I said. "Potential for some really nasty scandal here, if the cops and then the news people get to nosing around. Mostly involving a certain public figure, but it could easily splash onto the Company."

"Thanks for the consideration," he said drily.

"Hell," I said, "*I* don't want them opening an investigation either. If they poke around enough they might find out I was there today, and there's no telling what kind of ideas that could set off in their little brains."

There was another pause, this one a lot longer. Finally Griner sighed heavily. "All right," he said. "This is absolutely out of my department, you understand. None of this has a damn thing to do with me and I'm not even supposed to know you. Still and all, I'll get the word to the right people."

I said, "Leave me out of it, then. Find some way, I don't know, you got an anonymous tip or something. I don't want any suits coming around asking me questions. I went there today, she was dead when I got there, I left immediately and called you, period. I don't know a damn thing beyond that and I've had all the debriefing sessions I can handle for awhile."

A young guy came toward the phone, saw me using it, and hesitated. I shook my head at him and he walked away.

"I mean it, Griner," I said. "Keep them off my back, or I'll break the damn story myself."

"If it's the way you tell it, no problem. You didn't even call me. By the way," he said, "just how the hell did you get this call through on this line? You're not authorized—"

"I know," I said, and hung up.

That night at the hotel, I looked at the bed and knew there was no point in trying to sleep. The choices seemed to be to go out and get drunk in some bar or stay here and do it with the bottle I'd picked up on the way back from Silver Spring.

Stay here, I decided. Any bar I went into was odds-on to contain a slightly overweight brassy blonde with big ones, and I didn't need any reminders.

I set the bottle on the nightstand and went to get a glass. On the dresser beside the plastic-wrapped glasses (Sanitized For Your Protection) was one of those Gideon Bibles. I picked it up idly, thinking of Billy Jumper, wishing I could talk with him right now. The Bible fell open to the Psalms; I glanced at the page and saw:

> *Keep me, O Lord, from the hands of the wicked;*
> *preserve me from the violent man; who have pur-*
> *posed to overthrow my goings.*

I set the Bible back down, and then the glass beside it. Thinking about Billy Jumper had reminded me of something.

The little bag was down in the bottom of my suitcase, underneath my socks; I didn't even remember packing it, might well have picked it up with some other stuff. I never had used it or even looked at it since he'd given it to me.

I opened the bag carefully and poked at the contents with a finger, then sniffed. Some cedar in there, and what seemed to be some kind of sage, and other things I couldn't identify. There wasn't all that much of it.

Feeling faintly ridiculous, I poured the stuff into an ashtray and got a book of paper hotel matches. It took several of the flimsy things to ignite the mixture; the cedar seemed a little green. Once lit, however, it blazed up for a second, popping and crackling, before dying down to a smoldering glow. A surprising quantity of smoke billowed up from the ashtray. I wondered if this was going to set off the smoke alarm. Embarrassing as hell if it did; they'd never believe what I was doing.

I stood in the smoke, though, fanning it over myself with both hands, breathing it in, as Billy Jumper had advised. It had a pleasant smell; there was something in there that smelled oddly like butterscotch pudding, and the cedar and the sage touched off holiday associations. I found myself holding my hands in the smoke and rubbing them over and over each other, as if using the smoke to wash something away.

And maybe it was Indian medicine at work, or maybe I was just tired, but I stretched out on the bed and fell asleep and didn't wake up until morning. There were no dreams.

14
#####

DESPITE MY THREATS TO GRINER AND HIS ASSUR-
ances to me, I did have a brief encounter with the suits.
I suppose there was no way it could have been entirely
prevented. Certain things have to be done, whether there's
any point to them or not; it's how the machinery works.

They picked me up as the doctor finished checking out
how the bullet hole was healing; they were very polite as
they showed me to a small room and they promised this
wouldn't take long. It didn't.

It was obvious that they were merely checking off my
name on a list, written or otherwise, of people who were
to be interrogated concerning the recently deceased. They
asked, of course, if I had seen or heard anything down on
the island that might suggest any reason anyone might want
her dead.

I said, "Not unless it would be Jerry Raintree's wife."

They looked at each other. I wished I hadn't said that.
They chose to ignore my bad taste.

They also wanted to know whether Brenda had ever tried
to get any sort of information from me about the Company
or my own work. That struck me as an interesting question,
but I had to tell them no.

One of them—they'd given me names but I hadn't paid
attention; they were as interchangeable as a couple of

Mormon missionaries—said, "You do understand, Dane, you yourself are in no way under suspicion. She was dead before you ever got off the airplane from Texas."

"They got her while I was shooting it out with Ali and the gang?"

"Possibly not at the same time," the other one said, "but not long after, according to the autopsy. It's not impossible that she was killed *before* they went after you. Apparently the air conditioning slowed certain processes and it was hard to make an accurate determination of time of death."

I thought it was interesting that throughout the whole conversation they'd assumed I knew she was dead. Griner had told a little bit more than he was supposed to. At least I hoped that was how they knew I'd been there.

They didn't have any more questions for me. They said my discretion was appreciated, which I took as a gentle suggestion that I should continue to employ it.

I had another visitor at the hotel that evening. I was sitting there trying to decide what to do with myself until bedtime when there was a knock. I answered the door and there stood Vladimir Somov.

It actually took me a minute to recognize him. After all, I'd only met him the one time, and that under circumstances when I hadn't exactly been at my best. Then the recognition circuit closed and I said, "Son of a bitch. What are you doing here?"

He stood there in the hallway, one hand against the wall beside the door, giving me that sardonic smile. He had on a neatly-cut lightweight tan suit that definitely hadn't been made in Moscow.

He said, "I'm injured, Mr. Dane. One rescues you from a squalid fate in an emergent revolutionary state, then when one appears on your doorstep—so to speak—this is all you can say?"

I said, "Well, come on in. Want a drink?"

"That," he said, walking past me, looking about my room, "is, what is the idiom? More like it."

I held up the Jim Beam. "You drink bourbon?"

"With the greatest enthusiasm. And with nothing else, if you please." He took the bottle and looked at it while I went for glasses. "One of the finest products of the western democracies. We Russians with our hideous tasteless vodka, pfui! Whisky is for people who enjoy drinking," he said. "Vodka is for people who only want to shut off their minds and their senses because they live in a place too terrible to contemplate sober."

I handed him a glass and let him pour his own. "Strange talk from a KGB officer," I remarked.

"I'll tell you a joke," he said. "A man stands in line all day in Moscow to buy potatoes. When he finally gets to the head of the line they tell him there are no more potatoes. So he begins to shout and curse, and he says, 'What a hell of a country when you can't even buy potatoes!' And a big man comes over and says, 'Look here, *tovarishch*, I'm from the KGB, and you ought to be careful how you talk. Don't you realize only a short time ago you could have been shot for talking like that?' So the man goes home and his wife says, 'They're out of potatoes?' and he says, 'It's worse than that. They're out of bullets.' "

"Is that the one they're telling back home now?" I asked, taking the bottle back from him.

He shrugged. "How should I know? I haven't been there in years. The joke I heard on television the other night. Yakov Smirnov was on the Carson show." He raised his glass. "*Na zdorovye.*"

I poured myself one. Vladimir said, "The point is, as I keep reminding you, things are changing all over. And you might remember that the main reason Gorbachev was able to hold onto the reins of power at all was that the KGB chose to back him. After all, who knows better than we just how bad things are?"

I said, "Not to hurt your feelings again, Vladimir, but what *are* you doing here? Last I saw you, you were trying to make some sense out of the latest bungle in the jungle . . . by the way, whatever came of that business?"

"The people's revolutionary government has consolidated power and has formed ties with the ineffable Colonel Muammar Qadaffi. You will be delighted to learn that your old friend the Commandant was subsequently found guilty of counterrevolutionary activities and shot against the same wall where he executed so many others. It was said that he was made to endure a certain amount of pain before this happened."

I nodded. "I'll drink to that," I said, and did.

"As to my own presence here," he went on, "I'm now assigned to your own luxurious country. The rewards of many years of devoted service, and a certain mastery of that mixture of sycophancy and treachery necessary to advance in any bureaucratic organization. All perfectly legitimate," he said. "My status here, I mean. I am officially accredited to the Soviet embassy here in this extremely strange city— my God, how can the same country that produced bourbon and the Lincoln Continental also produce such hideous office buildings? But this call is purely a social one."

"How did you know I was in town?"

"Oh, come now." He looked at me over his glass. "Perestroika be damned, we haven't yet put bags over our heads. Your exploits down on that tiny island have aroused no small degree of admiration," he said. "If you should ever want to go to work for the KGB, I feel safe in offering you a generous contract. Ten men altogether—no, eleven, counting the Cuban pilot. Amazing."

"The pilot killed himself," I pointed out, "and one of the Arabs who was with him, when he tried to turn with too little airspeed and stuck a wingtip into the water. And one of the others, though you're not going to believe it, was killed by an Indian with a bow and arrow."

"Yes, we heard that." He shook his head and sipped his drink. "So it was a mere eight men you killed—two on one night, then six over the course of a single day. Somehow I remain impressed."

I shrugged. "I got on a roll, I guess."

"A charming expression. From the dice game, isn't it? At any rate." He finished his drink. "If you could possibly . . . thank you," he said as I handed him the bottle. "At any rate, thanks to your efforts, a tiny but very troublesome terrorist group no longer exists to any effective degree. Though they still have a few people scattered here and there, who will no doubt find other groups to join if they are not killed first. It is certain they will have learned nothing."

He turned the glass in his hands, looking at it. After a moment he said, "We didn't kill her, Dane. That was the chief thing I came here to tell you. If you will accept my word, we were not the ones who did it."

I set the bottle down and stared at him. "And why," I said, "did you think I might believe you did?"

He leaned back in his chair and studied me. "Is it possible," he said, "that you still don't known? Surely even the CIA has figured it out by now."

"They may have," I said. "They wouldn't necessarily tell me. Whatever it is you're talking about."

"She was working for us, Dane," he said, as if explaining something to a slightly slow child. "She was passing on information she got from Representative Raintree. Some of it was extremely useful information, I might add—you do realize he was on a committee which had access to classified material? Presumably she got him talking in the traditional way of her sort."

"Brenda was KGB?"

"No, no. Just a greedy woman who had something to sell and found buyers. She had, as far as anyone was able to learn, no ideologies or loyalties at all to handicap her. Which, incidentally, made her much more valuable; the closet Stalinists and desperate idealists are prone to taking risks, and are impossible to control."

I poured myself another one. The news was taking a little time to fit into my picture of reality. Well, now I knew why the suits had wanted to know if Brenda had ever pumped me for information. I could believe she'd given value for money. If Raintree was like every other Capitol Hill cowboy, he had a big mouth.

Vladimir said, "Unfortunately, she was too greedy. She began dealing with a second group of clients."

"The Arabs?"

"Even so. This city is alive with representatives of the radical Islamic world, you know—at times they almost outnumber the drug dealers. Everything from semi-legitimate diplomatic persons to professional secret agents to university students eager to aid the holy cause. There are even American citizens, either Muslim or simply crazy, who get involved in these things."

"And those who do it for money, I suppose."

"Some of these groups do dispose of impressive funds. I doubt if Abdelkader's heirs had much money to spend, but there are wealthy Arabs, and Arab governments, who would have bankrolled them."

"So Brenda was working for them too."

"How do you suppose they were able to get so much information on Mr. Raintree and his movements? How did they take those photographs and make those video recordings? And," Vladimir said, "how did you think they knew when he was going to be on the island? It was the opportunity they had been praying for, but they had to have inside information."

I remembered Cameron. "Somebody was talking about leaks," I said thoughtfully. "But my God, Vladimir, she could have gotten herself killed."

"Oh, I'm sure she had no idea what they planned. As you say, she would have been in great danger, and all I've heard suggests she was a very self-centered person. Besides, I don't think she would have been willing to get involved in something that extreme."

I shook my head. "No. I don't think so either."

"I suspect they intended to kill her," he said, "either during the course of the kidnapping or immediately after. She was of no further use to them and she knew too much. For one thing, she could have named her contacts in the Washington area."

I gulped my drink. Poor Brenda. Poor greedy dead Brenda. I said, "So you thought we might figure your people killed her. For working for the Arabs on the side."

"It is illogical," he said, "but you must admit your country-men have traditionally tended to make illogical assumptions where we are concerned."

"True enough," I admitted. "But then who did kill her? The Arabs?"

"It seems likely. As I say, there were still a few people here in Washington, and in New York, belonging to or affiliated with Abdelkader's group. I suppose they feared she might talk after they had failed in the kidnapping attempt. She may even have had some contact with them after her return; she might have been foolish enough to make threats." He sighed. "It is also possible that they somehow believed she had betrayed them, that this was why their attempt failed. When it comes to illogic, they are the world's grand masters."

He set his glass down and looked at me. "Of course, there are other possible suspects."

"The Company?" It had already occurred to me.

"Or conceivably the same people within it who were responsible for betraying you." Christ, he knew it *all*; I'd forgotten how good the bastards were sometimes. "Her association with Congressman Raintree created an ongoing security threat. They may even have found out that she was passing information to us. And it would not have been politic to try to pressure him into giving her up. . . ."

I thought it over. "I don't think so," I said. "It could be, but on balance I don't think so."

"You don't believe the CIA, or people within it, would be capable of doing such a thing? Come, Dane, we both know of cases—"

"Oh, sure. I don't really think they'd go that far when there were simpler ways of handling the problem, but they're capable of it. But it's not their style," I said. "An outright shooting, right next door to the capital, where an investigation by the police might turn up some dirt on Raintree? If they'd done it, there would have been no body. She would simply have vanished. Or else it would have been rigged to look like an accident."

He nodded. "I think you are right. Which leaves our Arab friends, it seems."

I thought suddenly about the crack I'd made to the suits about Raintree's wife. I remembered her pictures in the magazines: a nice high-class face, but a very strong face too, with eyes that had seemed to me to look right through any amount of bullshit. And she had the money to hire anything done that she might desire, and Brenda had been threatening both her marriage and her jackass husband's career. . . .

I said, "*Nah*," and Vladimir looked startled and said, "What?"

"Nothing," I said hastily. "Just thinking of something. No, you're right, it had to be the Arabs. Anyway, it's history. I'm not going on any avenging crusades. Hell, Vladimir, it's got to stop somewhere."

"Indeed." He stood up. "Let us have dinner some time before you leave the city. Are you going back to Europe?"

"Not any time soon. Looks like I'm out of the business for awhile, as far as the Middle East and Africa go." I stood up too. "There are still people who know I killed Abdelkader. I don't think any more of them are going to come after me in this country—although I'm planning to be damn careful—but I better stay out of their territory for now."

"Very wise." He moved toward the door. "What will you do? I would think a man of your talents would be able to find employment in a country like this."

"I imagine so." I followed him to the door. "Tell you the truth, I'd like to make enough money to buy myself an island like that one, somewhere. I kind of got to liking it there."

"That will take a great deal of money, I think. But no doubt you can do it. Find a generous employer," he said, his hand on the doorknob, "and if possible one who will not sell you out."

I nodded. "I'll tell you one thing," I said, "I'm through working for the Company. Free lance or any other way. It doesn't seem to agree with me."

He laughed. "But, Dane, my friend, how can you know? In our world, how do you ever know who is behind the people you think you are working for? Can you ever really know who your employers are?"

He opened the door, stepped into the hall, and turned back to look at me.

"After all," he said, "already you have worked for *us*, three times, and never knew it. . . ."